Susan Mitchell was born in Adelaide and began her career as a high school teacher there in 1966. After teaching in London schools for two years, she returned to the South Australian College of Advanced Education where she is now Head of the Literary Studies Department. She teaches scriptwriting for the media, women's literature and Australian drama. She has also worked for Crawford Productions as a scriptwriter and editor, for the ABC as their first television critic on *Today at One* and as presenter and writer of their radio programme, *The Coming Out Show*. She is the co-author (with Ken Dyer) of *Winning Women: Challenging the Norms in Australian Sport*, also available in Penguin.

Of the best-selling *Tall Poppies*, which is now a successful television series, critics have said:

'an engrossing book which should be required reading by all who care about Australia's future . . . Her pages crackle with life. They are also an education, worth a thousand turgid feminist tracts into what moves and concerns half the population of Australia.'

Tony Baker, Adelaide *News*

'good reading because the women never duck hard questions. In literature as in life, honesty becomes the best policy ... The pleasure of the book lies chiefly in getting to know closely women who are already household names.'

Edmund Campion, *Bulletin*

TALL POPPIES

Nine successful Australian women talk to Susan Mitchell

Penguin Books

Penguin Books Australia Ltd.
487 Maroondah Highway, P.O. Box 257
Ringwood, Victoria, 3134, Australia
Penguin Books Ltd.
Harmondsworth, Middlesex, England
Viking Penguin Inc.,
40 West 23rd Street, New York, N.Y. 10010, U.S.A.
Penguin Books Canada Limited,
2801 John Street, Markham, Ontario, Canada
Penguin Books (N.Z.) Ltd.
182-190 Wairau Road, Auckland 10, New Zealand

First published by Penguin Books Australia, 1984
Reprinted 1984 (six times), 1985, 1986 (twice), 1987, 1988, 1990

20 19 18 17 16 15 14 13

Typeset in Avant Garde by Dudley E. King, Melbourne

Made and printed in Australia by
The Book Printer

CIP

Tall poppies.

ISBN 0 14 007210 1.

I. Women — Australia — Interviews. I. Mitchell, Susan, 1945-

305.4'2'0994

Contents

For my Mother and Father

FOREWORD

For some people, the whole notion of 'Women of Achievement', implies elitism. Let me begin by saying that none of the women interviewed in this book sees herself as part of an elite, nor is she treated as such. None of them was born to success or had success thrust upon her. They did however achieve success through hard work, struggle and dedication. They made choices which were not always easy and which often caused them a great deal of conflict, but in each career that they chose to explore they blazed a trail for other women to follow. It's time we began to celebrate our 'tall poppies' and learn from the stories of their lives.

I collaborated with Susie on this book because I think there is a real need in our society to document the lives of successful women. Role models are extremely important and can be a great source of inspiration to other women at all stages in their lives. These personal anecdotal histories are compelling reading, not just because they answer that nagging question, 'How did these women do it?', but because of the extraordinary honesty and frankness which has revealed the women's many failures, struggles and doubts involved in making the choices they did. I was present at many of the interviews and this book is a testimony not only to the interviewer's skills but to the women who were brave enough to tell the truth.

Everyone who attains success has some spur, something that drives them on and makes them stand out above the rest. More often than not it comes from some sort of oppression, something that eats at them, some grain of sand that irritates enough to transform itself into a pearl. It can be said that merely being a woman in our society puts women behind in the race. The choice of gender is not theirs. Some women refuse to believe they were born at a disadvantage. Some, having recognised this, carry their belief like a crucifix and become bitter or hand-wringing. And some use it to their advantage, as a means to the end, which is to explore whatever talents they possess to their full potential.

Many of the women in this book started out facing extra obstacles. A Jewish refugee, a Yugoslavian migrant and an Aboriginal had to deal first with the prejudices of a society dominated by a white Anglo-Saxon culture. The point about all of their lives is that they have used that oppression. They have used their anger and frustration as a source of energy to achieve their own goals.

We live in a nation where the talents of half our population are not utilised. Women represent vast amounts of gold in Australia which for various reasons are not being mined. They are truly our most neglected resource. Most people accept that the economic and social role of women in Australia has undergone fundamental change in the course of our short history, but particularly in the last decade. Factors like maternity leave and increased opportunities for part-time employment have served to fuel a process which has seen the number of married women employed in the workforce expand from a trifling minority to a marked majority of around sixty-five per cent. Women, of course, have always worked inside and outside the home, particularly in times of labour shortage. However, unlike the aftermath of the Second World War when they were made to feel guilty and were sent back to their homes, this time they are in the workforce to stay. What is more, it is now generally agreed that in a society which aspires to be a meritocracy, they have as much right to be there as anyone else – in spite of the pockets of resistance to this point of view which still remain.

But just how fundamental have these changes been? Some would argue that they are not nearly as significant or far-reaching as this casual glance might indicate. In Australia, employment is still expected to be a secondary activity for a woman, secondary to the home, to the children, and to the husband's career. Though the working woman is increasingly becoming the norm, society itself has not altered in any fundamental sense to accommodate this changing role. What happens is that the working woman now has to bear the burden of two jobs, one paid and the other unpaid. Furthermore, the nature of female employment has altered surprisingly little in the course of this century. The labour market is still largely divided into separate male and female sectors with little overlap. Women remain concentrated in a small number of occupations, such as teaching, nursing and other caring professions, unskilled factory work, domestic service and minor office jobs. Virtually all of these vocations are simply extensions of the traditional female role. Women should no longer have to choose between being a wife and mother and having a career. No one ever expects a man to have to make that choice. Women must also be free to have their cake and eat it too! Not that I wish to denigrate any woman who chooses to be a full-time wife and mother. The point is that she chose it, society should not decide for her.

Freedom to choose is the touchstone of equality of opportunity. Any forces which threaten that freedom must be challenged and defeated. These interviews are living examples of women who have seized that basic human right to pursue their various talents in order to succeed in their chosen careers. I hope that by reading their stories all women gain a sense of their shared history and most of all begin to exercise their right to choose.

. . . nothing can take the place of persistence, determination – and a sense of your own worth.

Once having chosen it is important to remember the two qualities that all these women have in common – persistence and determination. There will always be stumbling blocks and pitfalls, moments of self-doubt and confusion. Think of these women, pick yourself up again and remember that nothing can take the place of persistence, determination – and a sense of your own worth.

Mary Beasley
Commissioner, Public Service Board of South Australia
Director, Qantas

INTRO-DUCTION

Australians have always liked to cut down their successful people, their 'tall poppies', especially when they consider they are getting too tall. It's often hard for successful men to avoid this fate – it's doubly hard for successful women.

Women have long been considered secondary to men, in their professional and their private lives, not because of so-called natural 'feminine' characteristics, but because of educational and social structures created and controlled by men. Despite this, some women have attained positions of professional excellence and are termed 'successful'.

How did these women succeed? At what cost? Are there any patterns that emerge? Is there a formula that others can follow? With these questions in mind I interviewed some successful women of different ages, classes, races and professions. Some of them are well-known public figures and some are less-known. They are all interesting and inspiring role models for other women who want to challenge and overcome their secondary status.

I knew none of these women personally before the interviews. I tried to see the world through their eyes and asked questions which I hoped would reveal the personal conflicts, agonies and motivations which lie beneath the public image of success. I have purposely kept the style simple and conversational. I want as many people as possible to read their stories. Here they speak directly and intimately to the reader as they did to me. There's an excitement about fitting all the pieces of someone's life together. I have stripped away the polite veneer which usually cushions conversations. The shock of the bare words is often hard to face. It was for some of the women interviewed. These nine women have had the courage to be this vulnerable. You have to be very brave to allow strangers to know you without your public masks in place.

These 'tall poppies' have all struggled to grow, refusing to be cut down, but it was easier for those with a strong self-image. In 1949 in her book, *The Second Sex,* Simone de Beauvoir emphasised the importance of how women were viewed and thus viewed themselves.

> 'What peculiarly signalises the situation of a woman is that she – a free and autonomous being like all human creatures – nevertheless finds herself living in a world where men compel her to assume the status of the other . . . How can a human being in a woman's situation attain fulfilment? What roads are open to her? Which are blocked? How can independence be recovered in a state of dependency? What circumstances limit women's liberty and how can they be overcome?'

These questions are just as relevant today. Too many women still make personal and professional choices as 'the other' rather than 'the one', the 'object' rather than the 'subject', the 'we' rather than the 'I'.

At what stage in our lives do we, as women, say to ourselves, 'What I want to do with my life is my number one priority – I am not a service centre for the needs of others'? Where does that will to succeed, that relentless persistence to explore your full potential come from? These interviews suggest that it is based in having a strong belief in yourself, in your own worth, a confidence in using the pronoun 'I'.

Some women seem always to have viewed themselves as subjects and acted on the basis of a strong self-image; others have been forced into assuming it through circumstances and necessity; others have had to achieve it through a process of painful choices. Whether the motivation was equality, necessity or autonomy – the three parts which make up this book – all of these women made their choices as 'the one'.

I am not suggesting that this is the key to success or that success can only be rated in professional terms. I do believe, however, that if more women want to become and survive as 'tall poppies', then these are some of the questions that we must each confront in our own lives.

Susan Mitchell

They always
assumed
EQUALITY

Treat these women as equals or face dismissal. These three women have always known that they were equal to anyone, if not better. They all have a strong sense of themselves and a belief in their ability to do whatever they choose. The sense of 'I' is always foremost. Although they understand how women can become victims they would never allow themselves to be treated in that way. All relationships, personal and professional, are conducted on the basis of equal exchange. There could never be any other way for them.

Beatrice Faust believes that biology largely determined what she became. Born a fighter and a rebel there was never any question of her being true to the beliefs and causes to which she was committed.

Eve Mahlab was expected to be independent from an early age. She has never hesitated in stating her own needs and fulfilling them. She believed that what was best for her must benefit her family.

Elizabeth Riddell simply trusted her own instincts and acted upon them. She never doubted that she could do anything she chose to do. Her life was something she organised to suit herself as well as others.

BEATRICE FAUST (Writer and retired activist)

On my way to interview Beatrice, the taxi-driver noticed my tape-recorder and asked me who I was going to see.

'A woman called Beatrice Faust – ever heard of her?'

'Oh yeah – women's libber type, isn't she?'

'That's the one – what else do you know about her?'

'Oh – a big beefy type of woman! Put it this way, lady, she's the kind of woman ya wouldn't want to meet on a dark night.'

I thanked him for his information. He wished me good luck.

The small woman in the brown cardigan who opened the door of the terrace house in Carlton introduced herself rather timidly as Beatrice Faust. As she led me upstairs to her little study, I boldly repeated to her the taxi-driver's remarks.

People tend to get a picture of me as a big person. One of the most common things that has been said to me for the last fifteen years when people are introduced is, 'Oh, but you're only little.' A friend who lived in this street with me for two years was six foot tall. I'm five foot two but it took him about twenty months to realise that he was taller than me. One cataclysmic day I was walking to the front door ahead of him. He saw me silhouetted against the light and said, 'By Christ, you're only little!' For some reason people are very naïve about size in relation to image.

I guess I've always been associated with things that were very touchy. I was talking about abortion in 1963 before it was trendy. I was talking about lesbians in 1969 before they were trendy. When one is associated with a whole lot of touchy subjects people get the idea that this person must be very hard-boiled.

Rebellion was part of my Irish background. I was brought up with a great deal of irreverence. My family has always had some sort of political connection – at least, my grandparents did. My grandfather was very hostile to conscription in the First World War, and very much in favour of things like the Commonwealth Bank and the Transcontinental Railways. Other people had to discover rebellion against their teachers and parents in adolescence, in a not necessarily intelligent way. It's a family story that the first money my grandfather ever made was on the Melbourne Cup and he lost it all on the 1916 Irish Rebellion. All this made it very easy for me to be agin the current stream. I rebelled by not being interested in adopting what my family considered to be a respectable profession. My father very much wanted me to learn to operate business machinery because after the war business was a big thing. That didn't interest me in the slightest. I actually developed a big block about typing. I learned to type when I was about thirty, because he had hounded me so much. He bought me a large, expensive typewriter as a sort of bribe.

I often terrify people by being very direct. It's not anything special in a man but it's not what you expect in a woman.

My family had a lot of Irish characteristics. My father married late, because in Ireland men marry late. His brothers lived with us because in Ireland families live in each other's pockets. My aunts lived next door. It wasn't the ordinary Australian suburban family constellation where the younger generation rebels against the older generation. In some ways I was not brought up.

My mother died when I was born. I had my father, two uncles, my aunt – a kind but retiring woman – and my stepmother who was very aggressive. She tried to manage the men, to stop them drinking too much and make them wipe their feet when they came in the kitchen. As far as I was concerned that was all just a terrible nuisance and very ugly. I mean, who cared about muddy feet on the floor? She did attempt to bring in a bit of feminine civilisation but it didn't work because all those men were too strong for her. I got used to the way men talk and relate to each other which again gives the impression that I'm 'big and beefy' because I often terrify people by being very direct. It's not anything special in a man but it's not what you expect in a woman.

I was different because my mother was dead and everyone else had mothers. I was different because I had a deformed chest. I had asthma and developed a caved-in chest from being unable to breathe. I didn't have to do sport at school. All the other kids had to get out and be sporting but I could sit and read books, which was a tremendous pleasure and relief. These things set me apart. I did know that I was very lonely. I spent a lot of time trying to figure out how not to be lonely, and how to learn to do things that would make me attractive to other children. I got on very well with grown-ups. I had a quite rich life but it wasn't the life of a child. I read about marvellous things in books which I didn't find in my own life.

Australian society was pretty limited in many respects before migrants got here. If you weren't born before or during the Second World War you can't imagine what the suburbs were like, though you can get some idea by seeing Barry Humphries on stage, or reading Patrick White novels and back copies of the *Women's Weekly*. At that time you had only one cinema where continental movies were shown. I can remember seeing *One Summer of Happiness* in which young teenagers run nude into the water. There was a terrible kerfuffle about the screening of a film with ninety seconds of nudity. I was naïve enough then to go to the Plaza to see a Japanese film called *Gate of Hell*. I went from school in my uniform and the woman at the ticket office said, 'I can't let you in to this movie, but if you go home and change your clothes and come back tomorrow afternoon, just pay your money and you'll get in.' So that's what I did.

The great thing for me was the coming of the migrants because they brought cosmopolitanism, different sorts of food, different movies, different attitudes, different clothes. They brought reality. In a certain sense the suburbs just weren't real. I can remember when we shifted houses, and took up the lino to find newspapers underneath with pictures of soldiers in New Guinea. It seemed to me that everything I read in the papers was more real and more human than what I could see around me: this terrible suburban deadness that you find in brick veneer, the roast lamb on the weekend. You couldn't say, 'Let's go to the beach,' in the middle of the week, because you didn't go to the beach in the middle of the week. Nothing could be done in a hurry. Everything had to be planned ahead and routine.

I was really going out of my head with boredom, with the absence of things that I read about: excitement and conflict and commitment. When the migrant kids began to arrive at school, bringing with them their often tragic, often very rich and wonderful backgrounds, I felt as if I had been brought into contact with reality for the first time. Because the early waves of migrants – called 'reffos' in those days – were usually the middle class or upper middle class people who had the money and the foresight to get out of Europe before things really blew up. They might have arrived here and eaten potatoes for six months because their qualifications weren't acceptable to the trade unions or the Australian Medical Association or something, but they were people who were multilingual. They knew English and they didn't have anything like the economic and social problems that the more recent migrants have. They could assimilate very well despite the hostility and the chauvinism which they met. Young people today don't realise what that group of 'reffos' brought to Australia and have no idea of the immense changes that took place.

Where other kids thought of them as 'reffos' who stank of garlic, for me they were just people from the Promised Land who had wide and rich experiences that I didn't have. Some of my first important friends were migrant girls. MacRobertson Girls' High School had a very high reputation in those days and a lot of it related directly to this influx of girls from fantastic backgrounds: multilingual girls who were highly motivated to get on academically, who had political interests and whose mothers had to work. Having a mother who worked was wonderful because these women were interesting. I often found that I got on better with their mothers than they did. To see women who were independent, educated and autonomous, and their

To see women who were independent, educated and autonomous, and their daughters growing up the same way, was wonderful.

daughters growing up the same way, was wonderful.

I wrote the usual schoolgirl things and I edited the school magazine. I imagine if you'd asked anyone in my class what was remarkable about me they would have said that I always came top and I had asthma and didn't do sport. That was my public image. Sex for me at that time was something very private. I have always had an immense fantasy life. I'd been masturbating to orgasm since I was very young, before I was three. I can remember crossing my legs in my high-chair and using the high-chair as a sort of brace. It was so much part of me it was like breathing. It wasn't something that I talked about because it didn't occur to me. I did once try to teach a little girl at school how to do it and she wasn't very successful. Just going through the motions of crossing your legs wasn't enough if you didn't have an inside impetus. I had it and she didn't. When sex became important as a teenager of course, I was an ugly duckling and very unconfident. In dancing class it was terrible to be amongst the last two girls to get a partner. You knew the partner you were going to get would be weedy, because all the nice boys came out from the sides of the hall in the first rush. I dropped out of dancing class very early because it wasn't teaching me how to get on with boys. I was very backward in terms of social sex. I mean, I'd never been kissed. In my matriculation year, it emerged that I was one of the only ones in my group who'd never been kissed, so there was a great campaign to get me kissed. It was just a matter of integrating my highly developed fantasy life into social sex later on.

I really loathed the narrowness of Australian life including censorship. I can remember *Love Me Sailor* when the prosecution was on. The penalty wasn't just a fine or having the book burnt; the author actually went to jail. My grandfather's view had been that the police should not be required to enforce moral things. As a policeman, he had a very articulate philosophy that the job of the police was to catch murderers and thieves. This background made it much easier for me to reject censorship and to find ways around it. It annoyed me very much to find that the sort of kids who'd gone to Geelong Grammar and whose parents had overseas holidays and two houses, had all the dirty books. They had no trouble getting them whereas you could never get them in a shop.

So I accumulated knowledge. I borrowed the dirty books. I

listened and talked. It became a matter of practical importance when my generation needed contraception and had to lie in order to get a diaphragm fitted: you had to say you were engaged otherwise you'd be thrown out. I didn't mind doing that – I mean, I felt I was cheating them, so up them! – but it was degrading to have to resort to subterfuge to get something that was really very, very practical and should be readily available.

In my environment abortion was considered a normal solution to a problem. One of the women in our street had three kids and her husband had a de facto who had three kids. This meant he was supporting six kids and two wives, one of whom had cancer. We all knew when the other got pregnant for the fourth time, and it was certainly agreed that she should have an abortion. It cost thirty pounds which was a fair whack for a housewife to pay out in those days. But it was a good abortion. It was done by a doctor and it was like having your appendix out. We all felt sorry, but agreed it was a good thing and very wise.

The censorship of sex in the media was such that until the First World War the reporting of divorce rates and abortion was very lurid. There was one sensational abortion case where a girl's body was washed down the Yarra in a yellow boot-trunk. The head was hung in a pickle bottle in the post office for identification. Then there was a blitz on reporting and divorces had to be reported in less than something like a hundred words. Abortion was a one-inch column and it was called an illegal operation. I always used to wonder what this 'illegal' business was because everyone was doing it – you know, if it was illegal why were these doctors doing it, why were these women having it? When I got pregnant I found out why. I had a terrible hoo-ha of doctors telling me I wasn't pregnant, that I had a period problem they were going to investigate. I kept saying, 'I am pregnant, I want an abortion.' They'd say, 'No, no you can't call it that because if the police come, we're all in trouble.' It seemed so irrational and so inhumane. I don't know what upset me more – the irrationality I think, plus the personal irritation of having to waste my time trailing around to these ridiculous people telling the same story over and over.

The first practical thing happened when a friend of mine said, 'Let's have a council for civil liberties and we'll fight various issues – you know, for Aborigines, vagrants thrown into jail for being drunk, and censorship.' So we convened a public meeting. We got a steering committee and civil liberties got off the ground in this State. I had an ulterior motive too because I'd been a member of the British Abortion Law Reform Association for some time and had been getting some marvellous literature. The British really know about politics. Girls who were born after the Second World War into this ridiculous grassroots, Maoist, Third World concept of politics don't understand real politics. We are not a Third World country. Grassroots are irrelevant in an industrial urban community. What you do is use constitutional means to achieve your ends. The British Labour Party did. It wasn't easy, and they still have trouble. But the way they went about changing public opinion, getting unions and women's groups behind them, taking opinion polls, accumulating evidence, doing cost benefits, surveys, and all sorts of things was simply magnificent.

I was a bit influenced by the American concept of civil disobedience: if the law is stupid the citizen has the right to disobey it and force changes. I couldn't find any doctors who were interested in civil disobedience. They just wanted to perform the abortion and get their money. Indeed we did get a little sub-committee to look into the abortion issue and a lot of material was accumulated but there wasn't much action. People were just not ready to go out on abortion at that time. They were ready to go out on censorship, Aborigines and vagrants, but not on abortion. It was basically puritanism. You could sit outside a doctor's residence or doctor's surgery and count the cars. You knew that there were a huge number of people having abortions.

It was kept illegal so that people felt guilty and therefore didn't want to talk about it. Instead of coming out and saying, 'Look, I've been robbed, I've been insulted, I've been raped,' what they did was try to forget it. This has been one of the immense liabilities in this country, worse I think than elsewhere. In France, with a strong Catholic background but with a more revolutionary attitude, you had 300 women signing the 'I have had an abortion, come and arrest me' statement. With all the work in the world in Melbourne I was lucky to get twenty-five women to sign saying 'I have had an abortion', go up to police headquarters and say, 'Come on arrest us! And we will make your life miserable for five years, because you're just never going to hear the end of it.' Of course nobody got arrested, but it came home to me very much on that particular little campaign just how timid Australian women were. Quite simply, our way of dealing with guilt is to forget it, to bury it.

It was only the generation in which most of the younger women hadn't had abortions that came into the campaign. They were there on principle, without the guilt and the timidity. They also had the immense model of the student revolt in America, the riots at Berkeley and Kent State Universities. They had inherited a whole political tradition from the anti-war movement and the black civil rights movement which, although not really relevant to us as women, at least showed us how to get organised.

I have learned painfully over the years that I am not a good committee person. I have strong feelings and original ideas but I am not the sort of tactful manipulator who fits well into committees – you know, you run up a hell of a phone bill and you spend a lot on stamps but there's not a great deal to show for it. I spent a lot of time trying to amend my personality, to learn committee skills and assertiveness. Then I decided, 'Well look, for ten years I've tried to make myself a committee woman and it doesn't suit, so I'll give up. I'll stick to writing, which is what I'm better at.'

Abortion really became a media issue in 1966. Before then there'd only been articles, conferences and seminars. Two things happened. The House of Lords passed the first abortion bill in England. Probably three or four bills before that had not got through. Also at that time there was television which was not bound like the newspapers to one-column inch descriptions of 'illegal operations'. Because they were making their own rules, they just said, 'To hell with all this crap, an abortion is an abortion, we're going to say it on television. If people don't like it they can turn it off.' It took off then as a media issue because television led the way and the newspapers followed.

I did get an immense thrill out of public speaking. It's like acting when you get a rapport with the audience and you know, 'If I do it this way they'll laugh, if I do it that way they'll shut up, and if I do it some other way they'll stand up in their seats.' There is certainly that 'smell of the greasepaint, roar of the crowd' feeling. It's not the same with television, because you're facing a whole lot of electric wires and blank machines with little faces peering out at you from under their earphones. I found television was not something that I could do very well.

My main interest was in seeing change. I wanted the law changed. What I had to do to get that, or what I exposed myself to was more or less irrelevant. I did get knocked back for jobs. I suppose there were half a dozen occasions in my life when I had discrimination because of my reputation and because of my activities. That annoyed me too of course. It was precisely that sort of thing I was fighting.

My father died and left me a small income. If I had to earn my living I would be doing very badly. It took me a long time to learn to handle money. This created an immense resentment in me because I knew money was power, but my family handn't taught me how to save or how to use money at all. It took me probably ten years of very conscientious effort to get that under control, to learn how to spend and how to save, how to invest and how to budget for your taxes. I've always had a secret feeling of shame that I've never managed to make myself self-sufficient. A lot of the time I have been supported by either my father's money or, more recently, my husband's money. I realise now that it's ridiculous to be ashamed when my husband earns about ten times as much as I do. Unless I radically change what I want to write and what I want to sell, I will never earn that sort of money. He is quite generous and in the last three or four years I've become much less guilty about taking his money. I'm not so stroppy about paying for things myself or making sure that the budget is equitably divided between us. It's just not an issue with me any more.

I first married when I was twenty. That relationship, with living together before marriage and marriage, lasted just over two years. It was very formative because my first husband was a highly intellectual person and very well trained in research, in thinking and reading and getting to the bottom of things. For a long time after we broke up people would say at parties, 'Oh, you must be Clive Faust's sister because you argue just the same way that he does.' Quite a few people got upset because I used the methods of argument that I'd learned from him. He was twenty-six and older in some ways, certainly intellectually. Socially, he had some of the problems that many

Australian men do, and that didn't make for an easy life between us.

My single name was Fennessy which goes back to the Irish background. When I was born my father was distraught because my mother died twelve hours later. He was unaware that she had died and when the doctors finally got on to him he was terribly upset. Then they said, 'You've got to register the baby and you've got to put a name down – what are you going to call it?' And he said, 'Find out what her mother was called and call her that.' So that's how I got Beatrice. He never forgave me for her death. Faust has been a good name to have published and publish under, but it wasn't formative in any sense because it came to me very late, and it wasn't mine anyway. I made it mine by publishing and writing and speaking. I feel now I've got as much right to it as anyone.

In some ways, I resent the fact that I was not forced to do sciences when I was at school . . . I ended up doing Arts which was pleasant and easy and, of course, not marketable.

I married when I was in third year of an honours Arts course which was very broken up due to ill-health and marriage and mismanagement. It took me six years to recover my position, or rather three years after third year. My main thing after the marriage had broken up was to get my degree and just stay afloat. By the time I had my degree, my father had died and left me enough money to be a little bit independent. I did a second degree purely out of pleasure. Doing the MA was wonderful because I was not constrained by courses, or by people's concepts of what I should be doing, and a lot of obligatory work that was really dead. In a way, having the money was bad for me because it meant I could fool around in things like civil liberties when I should have been thinking about getting a job and a marketable skill. I mean, a degree in English literature is not marketable really. In some ways I resent the fact that I was not forced to do sciences when I was at school. I was good all round and if I'd bothered I could have done medicine. I had toyed with the idea of medicine but I ended up doing what was pleasant and easy and, of course, that was not marketable.

Germaine Greer and I both got 2A degrees. We were both told, 'It should have been a first but . . .' Basically we both knew that if the examiners had wanted us to have firsts they would have given a few extra marks here or there but they didn't. With a 2A you can't go anywhere. Germaine of course recovered herself brilliantly. She went to Sydney and to England. I didn't. I mucked about too much, so I effectively cut myself off from university teaching. I regret that because I think I would be happy in a university environment where it is possible to lead an intellectual life where you read and talk and have leisure to think about what's happening, and you're not under the sort of nine to five pressure where you don't have time to think.

A lot of my friends were teachers and they were highly committed. I see them now, in middle-life, disgusted with the education system here and trying wildly to find some way to change their careers at a time that's economically very unpromising, though some of them are successfully moving into other areas. These were people who went in with ideals, who wanted to do something for kids, for migrants. They spent many rich years trying to change things and then got beaten down.

One of the first things that hit me when I was in high school was Aborigines. I went to the Inter-schools Christian Fellowship. I was also a member of a church that ran missions in Western Australia. The poverty and discrimination against Aborigines was just appalling. I remember saying to the lady who led the Inter-schools Christian Fellowship, 'What are we going to do? I feel as if I should be making some sort of sacrifice and getting up and doing something.' She gave me a realistic answer which was that it wouldn't do any good if we all lived like Aborigines. I was just horrified that a sweet, Christian woman, who I'm sure was quite humane, was giving me this ridiculous non-answer. When I hit university there was a group which was committed to raising money for Aboriginal tertiary scholarships. I can see now that it was starting at the wrong end, but at least it was something.

It was also very evident that the politicians were not doing anything about sex education, contraception and abortion. I'd always felt that you ought to be able to lean on these people and tell them what the public want. The first dry run I had was called Parliamentary Abortion Lobby and lasted six months. I wanted to start off doing the sort of things that had been done in England. The first thing was to find an exact register of what every member of parliament thought. I tried to organise a whole lot of people into cells for writing and compiling letters and getting breakdowns so you knew exactly what your support or opposition was in parliament. Unfortunately at that time the grapevine I was into consisted of medical students who were all heavily burdened with their courses. I did get some help and began to build up a picture, but it fizzled out because they just didn't have the time to devote to it. It wasn't something I could sit down and do all by myself.

Then the women's movement started to take off. I was interested in seeing things happen to women and I knew a women's movement would be interested in abortion. At that time, somehow or other I picked up a copy of *Ms* magazine which had a whole series of interviews with the presidential candidates when McGovern and Nixon were running. The interviews compared the candidates' views on women with the number of women employed in their campaign committee, and compared the treatment and pay of those women with that of the men. Of course, American politics are much more sophisticated, and although they had more money and staff, it seemed to me that we ought to be able to do something. Because the women's movement grew out of the American new left, there was all this nonsense about grassroots. Nobody was interested in members of parliament because – you know, that was old fashioned, they were repressive capitalist democracy. So having touted the Abortion Lobby idea round the women's liberation groups, I thought, 'Well, there are other women who are interested in women's matters who are appalled by women's lib., who just think they're juvenile and that they're not going to do anything practical. They talk too much and act too little.'

There are women who are interested in women's matters who are appalled by women's lib., who just think they . . . talk too much and act too little.

I realised there was a whole group of women not being reached by women's liberation who were in fact being turned off because of the irrelevancy of all the student rebellion crap and the Reichian-Marxist-Freudian politics. Reich! Dreadful influence on politics! So I tried to tap those women that I knew and the people I'd known through civil liberties, to reach a different group of women. They were indeed there, and they did indeed respond. Every meeting the group just grew. Initially I started off with just ten people, then there were fifty and then there were 120. It grew astronomically and it happened to be 1972 when there was obviously going to be a change of government. We were very lucky because there was intense excitement and activity going on in all directions and an optimistic feeling that things were happening. We were one of the things that were happening. In a quite real sense, for the first six months I carried a lot of the shitwork myself and did all the roneoing and typing. But in another sense all I did was provide an idea for women who were looking for that outlet. Of course, if it hadn't been for the women and their readiness, nothing would have developed. It would have fizzled out. In some ways, it was just extraordinary luck that it happened in 1972 and that there were women available.

When we started The Women's Electoral Lobby (WEL), I recognised the validity of a lot of things women's liberation was saying about hierarchical structures and women's ability to use groups. I respected the value of a certain cooperativeness rather than a hierarchy. We tried to organise WEL in a series of cooperative committees that were interlinked but small enough to give people self-expression and experience and let everyone contribute. I came to the conclusion that if you are too different from the community in which you are working you don't interface with them. This was painfully obvious with women's libbers. They could not interface with the community they were living with. There was a schizophrenia about getting money from the government at the same time as hating the government. You can't have it both ways, and rapidly I came to reject the belief that cooperativeness was the way to do it. Human life is just not long enough to organise things in those ways. It's all right if you're a Christian and you can think Heaven and God will carry you through, but for real politics you can't afford to be disorganised like that.

I regretted very much having to give away those ideas so I drifted out, and I personally wasn't right for that sort of thing as my own personal experience in the abortion campaign which followed WEL led me to believe. I knew that there were women who wanted a women's movement that was not dominated by women's liberation and four-letter words and radical lesbians and know-it-alls and demonstrations. They didn't want to demonstrate: they wanted to change things.

I always knew that my main interest was abortion and abortion led to contraception, contraception led to sex education, sex education led you back to censorship. There are still sex education books that are being seized by censorious people. Sex education books that are banned by such people can't be used in schools. I didn't want to impose my abortion interests on all these women. I felt that in that climate you could be discredited if you were identified with abortion, because I'd already had some personal trouble. It seemed to me that it would handicap WEL in the sort of things they wanted if you came out on the strong abortion platform. Most of these women were sympathetic, but it wasn't their primary interest. It seemed to me tactful to withdraw my abortion interests out of WEL. That was a political pragmatic decision. Once Labor was in office and there was a possibility of legislation, I became President of the Abortion Law Repeal Association. It had been the Abortion Law Reform Association but when I got in we changed it to 'Repeal'. I put most of my work into that for sheerly tactical reasons. I was delighted to see how well WEL was doing without me because it meant that things were going as I'd hoped. After fighting the abortion things and wrecking my car and wrecking my bank account and deciding that I just wasn't a committee person, I got out.

I remarried in 1969. We don't keep anniversaries. It might have been 1970. We lived together for a while before marrying. So marriage just doesn't have that epoch-making quality for me. At one stage the front room was devoted to the office for the Abortion Law Repeal Association. Pregnant women were coming from New Zealand wanting abortions and people were ringing from interstate. It was quite mad. Shane was amazingly patient considering the phone calls and hassles.

He got a bit shitty at one point about stamps. I used to give him heaps of letters to post and because I didn't discriminate between my needs and the campaign I would just spend my own money. I've got no idea how much money I spent of my own. One day, after he had been taking these bundles of letters to the post office, he decided he wasn't going to bankroll its postal expenses any more – but that was the only point of friction. I think it was just a passing irritation – you know, you get to a moment when you blow up. I've had much less friction than some women. I knew one woman whose husband ripped the phone out of the wall after the twenty-seventh call during dinner. You have to live with this. I don't know how the suffragette generation managed. I think they were really blessed in not having all that many telephones.

Once you get a movement going and are making news, the media want you. Students of sociology would want to do a case study on an organisation. I'd say, 'Here's the organisation. It's one telephone, a piece of wood and two packing cases.' I reckon that there've been more people interviewing, studying, writing essays or doing projects, than have ever worked for WEL. We've got some sort of ridiculous stage where half the community is parasitic on the voluntary efforts of the other half. It looks as if we would rather study social change than make it happen. I can live with that now. It used to make me very annoyed. If only these people put their energies into working for social change instead of writing about it, we'd have a lot more to show. I guess that it's just one of the things of our time.

If only these people put their energies into working for social change instead of writing about it, we'd have a lot more to show.

The more I study the history of feminism and look at what women achieved with much less money and much less resources it amazes me. I guess it's because their own lives were rather simple. They didn't have the media on their backs, or people studying them, and they didn't have the telephone, so they were able to lead fairly normal lives at the same time as working for their various causes.

WEL was 1972–3 and abortion was about 1973–5, and from there I went into freelance writing to try and earn pin money. I wrote for *Nation Review* from its inception, which was good because there was immense freedom to say what you thought. In another way it was not good because it wasn't reaching the widest possible audience. I really dislike preaching to the converted. You've got to get the audience which is not yet converted, either the silent majority or the opposition. When I wrote *Women, Sex and Pornography* I deliberately chose a level of simplicity which I thought would reach a large number of people. There's a lot of academic background behind it but that's not the foreground of the book at all. I made it conversational and simple. I tried to reach the sort of audiences that I get in College of Advanced Education lessons and parent teacher meetings, the sorts of groups who invite me as a public speaker.

I regret having done a lot of journalism because now I'm writing books I find I'm behind with the style. I always tried to imitate Orwell. At intervals I've gone back to Orwell and studied him carefully. But when it comes to actually writing, things happen. You get rung up at eleven o'clock and asked, 'Can you get to the ABC at half past eleven to see a preview videotape of this or that and review it?' Under those conditions it's impossible to sit down and develop a graceful style. I regret that very much at my time of life. Now that I've done a hell of a lot of writing, I don't feel I've got a personal voice. I'd like to be like Galbraith. He's so brilliant in making complicated things simple. If I could combine the virtues of Galbraith and Orwell I would be very pleased. I don't get a thrill out of reading what I've written. Beatrice Faust the political activist? Well, she's retired. In fact, when people say, 'Give me three lines for a biographical note,' I've started putting 'activist – retired'.

This is the other great thing about having money. Most women give labour and give time because they don't have money to give. I really think that it would be much more constructive to run a restaurant or make dresses or do anything, even take a job typing, so money can be donated for things to be done professionally with the bankroll behind them. I have enough money and my husband doesn't mind me not contributing to the household. I can write a cheque if I want to. I really feel that I'm doing more that way than I would be wearing myself out running around ringing people up, begging for this and that and going into this terrible drudgery of what politics really are all about.

I've got a teenage son but he's fairly privileged. The university crèche was being established around the time he was born which was very convenient. Due to marrying a tolerant, well-educated, white-collar worker, I was able to send him to private school. I was disappointed in having to do that because in principle I don't believe in the two-school system. In my day there were a couple of high-ability high schools for the number of teenagers who wanted to go into tertiary education and they were just about adequate. You no longer have those choices. I just looked around and realised that unless I was prepared to buy a house near a good high school, the simplest thing to do was to send him to a private school. I didn't want to spend all my life on mothers' clubs. That was another decision I made very early on. A lot of my friends were sending their kids to state schools and were breaking their hearts doing the mothers' club routine. I really feel that one of the quickest and most beneficial things you could do would be to pull all the women out of all the voluntary work. I think voluntary work is a social disaster. These wonderful hard-working mothers with two or three kids who do fantastic jobs never get recommended for anything. They never get OBEs. When was the last time you saw the president of the state school mothers' club get an OBE or a Damehood or whatever?

You've got to start with the pregnant women. Education goes back to having healthy children who can speak well and have language.

My approach to the educational problem would be quite simply that you've got to start with the pregnant women. Education goes back to having healthy children who can speak well and have language. It's very clear that kids brought up in overcrowded situations do not acquire language sufficient for our community. Listening to alternative educationalists like Ivan Illich and Paulo Friere has been a disaster. It's all very well to say that people in the Third World countries learn to read by reading traffic signs, but what they can read is not very substantial. In this world of microchip technology you have to be able to read polysyllabic words. You have to be able to count more than from one to ten. You can do that on your fingers. If I were Pope I would immediately cut off all funding from tertiary institutions and tunnel it into the care and nurturing of pregnant women and children under five. Pump all the money in at the beginning because once you get to high school it's too late, the kids are wrecked! That's another reason why I got out of teaching. The first time I taught I was fairly ruthless. I just did what I'd seen my own teachers do and it seemed to work. The second time I taught migrant kids and poor kids who had monumental problems. In probably seven out of ten state schools a teacher had to be a social worker as well. It was soul destroying and not doing the kids or the teachers any good. What we should be doing is preventing these problems before they become as chronic as they are.

The sooner women learn to respect each other's individual differences the more chance the women's movement has of getting lasting change.

My main book is called *Apprenticeship in Liberty*, sub-titled Sex, Feminism and Sociobiology. I think there are biological sex differences. We should recognise them. There is nothing that can be said about women's biology that can't also be said about men's biology. Biology, far from being rigid and constraining, is varied, flexible and liberating. We should use it to be liberated with.

Feminism has buried its head in the sand. For example, the Equal Rights Amendments look like collapsing in America. There are many reasons for it. One reason is that the women's movements have simply failed to look at the average housewife, who is very often black and poor, or a struggling white. They've messed it up because they're too middle class. They've missed out the fact that a lot of women genuinely enjoy motherhood and bringing up kids. If you threaten that enjoyment which is really fulfilling for them, then they will reject you and your programmes. This is a tactical mistake that was also made by the suffragettes. Now it's been made again it's worse because we won't get a second chance. The sooner women learn to respect each other's individual differences the more chance the women's movement has of getting lasting change. This means respecting the right to be a radical lesbian on the one hand or a dedicated mother on the other. Mothering must be respected.

It's painful to read feminist history, and discover that everything that has been said since, say, 1963 has all been said before. It's been forgotten and our generation is having to say it all again. But I don't think that what I'm saying about biology and accepting the flexibility of biological differences has been said before. I think people have been frightened by biology. They use it for conservative purposes or they've ignored it. The women's movement is running scared and has its head in the sand as far as that goes. To me it is fascinating. No one taught me to like sex, or to have orgasms when I was little. Nobody taught me to fight, it just came. I know there are boys who fight and there are boys who are sissies. There are girls who fight and there are girls who are gentle. I was one of the tomboys. Looking back on my own experience I'm quite sure that this is a biologically based phenomenon. It applies equally to boys as to girls. You've got to say that temperament cuts across sex barriers, temperament is biologically based. We need flexible roles to allow for a full range of temperaments. It's as simple as that.

Beatrice went downstairs to see a friend who had called in. I looked around the small room which was crammed with books, magazines and bulging folders. Having just talked with her for nearly three hours, I now understood how a short woman with a caved-in chest from chronic asthma can give the impression of a large, aggressive woman. What is projected is not just the strength of her beliefs but her sense of herself.

The phone rang and then stopped. Someone downstairs had answered it. I noticed that the phone on her desk had a sheet of paper taped to it. I leaned forward to get a closer look at the writing on the paper. The message read, 'No. I have a dead-line to meet.'

She's clearly as tough on herself as she is with her opponents. Similar pieces of paper with notes to herself were taped to the bookshelves. The one above her desk read, 'What am I trying to say? Have I said it? What image or example would make it more vivid? Avoid padding.' I quickly copied it down for future use.

ELIZABETH RIDDELL (Journalist and poet)

Picking my way through the lush growth of camellias and azaleas, I climbed carefully down the slippery slate steps and rang the bell.

Relaxed and casual in jeans and a jumper Elizabeth welcomed me into her sitting room. We drank coffee and chatted. The cat dozed on the hearthrug in the morning sun.

Despite her warmth and charm, there was a sharp glint in her eyes that told me she didn't suffer fools gladly. I knew there would be no point in pussy-footing around. My questions were straight and to the point. Her answers were tough and totally lacking pretension or humbug. She didn't pull any punches when talking about her own life. She even admitted to lying about her age. 'I always say I was born in 1910 – even that's bad enough. But I think I have 1907 on my passport . . .'

I never think. I'm not logical or analytical. I listen. A little bell goes off in my head and says, 'Do' or 'Don't'. Everything I've done in my life has been by instinct.

I never had any doubt that I could do anything. Perhaps that was from my childhood. I always knew I was going to be a writer but I didn't know I was going to be a journalist. I had been published by the time I was eleven. At school I wrote the sort of poetry which I'd read. Copying Sir Henry Newbolt – that was my style. I wrote very bad poetry for the New Zealand magazine, *Freelance*, which didn't pay me. They didn't know who I was but they published it. I used to write a poem for every great occasion and send it to *Freelance*. I was at boarding school you see and they didn't know. I was never paid for anything until I came to Australia. Ezra Norton, the editor of *Truth* and the *Daily Mirror*, came on a fishing expedition to New Zealand to recruit talent. I was in my last year at school. He hired me and I was thrown into Sydney journalism. I'd never thought that you could make your living in writing except as a journalist.

My father was drowned in a yachting accident when my sister was six and I was four. He was an accountant and left nothing but debts. My mother was trained to give nice dinner parties, not how to make a living, so she sold the house, put us right up north in Auckland with old and quite well-off relatives, and went to work selling insurance. She had a lot of charm and of course that is the thing that is necessary in selling. She supported us like that. Then she took up selling advertising and was absolutely marvellous at it. She was able to send us both to boarding school and to have a good time herself and lots of lovely clothes. Sometimes we'd have bad months when she hadn't sold much or hadn't bothered to. She was an extraordinary woman for her day and age and background, which was upper middle class of the worst sort – missionaries who stole the land from the Maoris and so on. She was like me. She didn't think. Because if she thought, it was all too awful. So she just went and did things.

I never had any doubt that I could do anything . . . I always knew I was going to be a writer.

I had no friends at school. Being alone didn't worry me. Although I was not a Catholic I went to a convent. It was supposed to be good for discipline. I think I was a difficult child for my mother. I didn't get on with my sister so we were sent to different schools. I didn't know I should have friends. When I hear of people who have retained school friendships I haven't the faintest notion of what that is about. I lived in my head. Even in the holidays. There were no boys in my life . . . I just read. And I stuttered terribly badly. To cure me a nun told me to take Palgrave's *Treasury* out into a paddock. She said, 'Go and sit in the paddock and read. Don't read for the punctuation, just read in a monotonous voice.' And it worked.

My world was full of romantic history. I read novels about England and knew every English street by heart. We had a marvellous school library. I don't think the nuns knew what was in some of the books. I didn't do any mathematics or science. When my mother changed her mind and said perhaps I could matriculate, I failed. I came top in Christian doctrine, English, history and geography. I was hopeless at anything else. I only wanted to know what I wanted to know. That's fatal in school life. Mother told me she couldn't afford to send me to university and that I had to get a job. Then the offer from Norton turned up, and she let me go – the great thing that mothers can do for their children. All the family said, 'She can't go to Australia, wicked Australia.' Oh yes, New Zealanders think, or thought then, that Australia was a hotbed of sin. I was eighteen.

I was offered a job on *Smith's Weekly* for another pound a week. I leaped at that. I was working with Kenneth Slessor, Colin Simpson and Colin Wills, my ideal writers.

My employers gave me a proper wage and for the first two weeks they paid for me to stay in a little bed and breakfast place in Macleay Street. Then I was on my own. I adored it. I was fascinated by Sydney. Everybody was terribly nice to me. I was thrown into doing film and theatre reviews about which I knew absolutely nothing. I wasn't given any training; I was simply told, 'Go out and do it. We want this many words and get it in on time.' That meant coming back to the office after the play at eleven-thirty to write the copy.

I left that first paper because I was offered a job on *Smith's Weekly* – a famous old weekly paper – for another pound a week. I leaped at that. I was working with Kenneth Slessor, Colin Simpson and Colin Wills, my ideal writers and all handsome men – well, Ken wasn't handsome. I sat in an office with them at *Smith's Weekly* and between us we reviewed films and books and wrote stories about features. They taught me everything. We all ate our sandwiches together, and went to the pub on the corner. At that time I was living in a series of little flats in Macleay Street.

Then I met Ted (Edward) Greatorex, known as Blue – a tall, handsome, red-haired journalist. I fell violently in love with him. I took a nice flat at Darling Point and he moved in with me. Blue was a good journalist but he wasn't as good as I was, which he freely acknowledged. He was absolutely marvellous to me. He didn't ever want me to stop being a journalist and always encouraged me. He didn't want a wife and children. He wanted a girl and a lot of fun. And we didn't interfere with each other too much. Sometimes we worked against each other on stories. He was extraordinarily good about that. I never saw myself as a mother, so it was a good thing I didn't have any children.

In 1935 we planned to go to England. We found we couldn't get a cabin together because we weren't married, so we got married. I didn't mind, but I don't think he wanted to get married. He was very interested in women. But he said, 'Well, we'll have to get married.' So off we went to England on a cargo boat. As soon as we arrived Blue got a job with a newsagency like Reuters, called Exchange Telegraph. He was sent on a tour of test matches. I wrote to every editor in London saying who I was and what I was. I got a letter from the *Daily Graphic* offering two days' work a week. When I asked why I was offered the job I was told, 'Oh, Australians don't know when they're being snubbed – they just ask questions. And they don't go to the back door – they go to the front door.' The *Daily Graphic* gave me a very good run – bylines and things. I also did a bit of work for the *Daily Express*. They had a William Hickey column run by Tom Driberg, who became a great Labour Party man, and he used my work.

We led independent lives and we never questioned each other about what we were doing. I don't know how it worked, but it did.

My ambition was to get on the *Daily Express* as it was the most glamorous and successful daily in England then. I went to see the editor all the time who kept saying, 'No, no. I don't want anybody like you. I want to find a wonderful girl who's never done any work and make her into a star.' He couldn't find her so he reluctantly put me on at the basic Fleet Street wage. These editors really were prima donnas. Every morning his secretary would pin up a notice that he had dictated, saying how we'd made fools of ourselves. It would say something like, 'I never want to see in the *Express* a phrase such as, "a ship limped into port",' and everybody would cringe, especially the sub-editor who had let that go through. I got a very good run but eventually he found his girl, and off I went.

I nearly had a nervous breakdown from horror that I'd been sacked. I'd only been there ten months. I went home crying to Blue. He said, 'All right, let's get out of this place, we'll go where its warm and nice.' So we lived in Spain for three months. We came out when Franco came in. Our waiter at a pub where we used to eat became a commissar. He warned us that there was going to be trouble, so we stayed there just long enough for us both to get a story out of it. The British sent a boat to get all the British off the Costa Brava and we went out with them. I went back to England and worked wherever they would have me. I'd recovered from the shame of being sacked. We worked and we had lots of friends. We didn't have any Australian friends except a very well-known writer called Max Murray, because I hadn't come to England to have Australian friends. We bought a little car, toured everywhere and had a very good time.

We came back to Australia in 1939 by another slow cargo boat. I got a job on the *Sun* and they were going to send me away to do something but then the war broke out. Blue was about ten years older than I was, and he didn't want to be in the war. But when France fell he got peculiar and said, 'I'll go to the war, to save France.' He went into the army and then into the airforce, but he never got out of Australia. He was in the Eighth Army Division. If he'd stayed in it he would have been sent to Changi or the Burma Road. Fortunately he got into the airforce. He began as a sergeant in the army, and he ended the war as a squadron leader in the airforce. I was sent to open the New York bureau of the *Daily Mirror*. Men couldn't leave the country. Journalists could go into the army if the proprietor let them. If they were not key men in the newspaper industry they could go as correspondents, but you couldn't have sent a man out to open up a bureau. I asked Blue, 'Do you mind if I do this? He said, 'No, I'm in the airforce going up to New Guinea.' He put airforce friends in our Vaucluse house. He never stopped me from doing anything. He may not have wanted me to go, but I took this at its face value. Besides I wanted to go.

So I left him for three years. I was in touch with him all the time. We wrote to each other and he never said a harsh word to me. He no doubt made other arrangements. So did I. You didn't know when you were going to be killed, so you lived your life as if it was your last day and night. I dare say everybody did the same. I used to work twelve hours a day in New York. It was a very hard job. I was the only person in the bureau. I didn't even have a typist. I had a typewriter and a teleprinter and that was all. Eventually I got sick of it and asked to go back to England. America was a silly place to be in the war. If the war was on you might as well be where it was happening.

I went over to London on a convoy. I'm very bad about dates but I can tell you the date of that – 1944, the little blitz. We were all waiting for the invasion, but then we got the doodle-bug. During that time I went up north and to Ireland, finding out about immigration. The whole of the United Kingdom was totally disturbed by the war. The people were not going to put up with the things they'd put up with from previous British governments. The women of England had been exposed to all these marvellous men – the Poles, the Canadians, the Australians, the very free French – and they were not going to be told what to do by their husbands, lovers or fathers again. The whole thing was a ferment. I wrote a lot about that, waiting for the invasion, and I wrote a lot of my best poetry during the war. I was also writing serious stuff about Britain, but nobody in Australia believed me. They printed it because they were told to.

I got sick of the war. I felt it was worse to be on the winning side than on the losing, in a way. So I went to Paris where it was very hard at first because there was no electricity, no transport, you had cold water in the bath and were living on army rations. Things improved when Eisenhower made his headquarters there. The American army always makes itself comfortable. I'd seen refugees everywhere. Geoff Hutton of the *Age*, a Canadian girl, and I, got a driver and set off for Strasbourg. We were interested in seeing Malraux, the writer. On the way we went through Nancy where there was a press camp. All the journalists were there with their feet up on their desks reading the unexpurgated version of Lawrence's *Lady Chatterley's Lover,* which they'd bought in Paris, and all the Henry Miller books. They were all writing pieces that began, 'Today I saw the death of the German army . . .' and it wasn't dead by any means. At Strasbourg, the German army was just across the river. When we returned through Nancy the press camp had gone. The German army had revived and driven them back. We headed back for Paris in a jeep, in uniform. We were in great danger, terrified out of our wits, thinking, 'If the Germans catch us, they won't stop to ask us who we are, they'll kill us.' However, we got there safely. Then we went to Ravensbrook which had been a concentration camp. Not one German around Ravensbrook admitted that there'd ever been a camp or guard-dogs or even an electrified wire. It was disgusting. But the Germans were having a bad time too. They were apologising for themselves and explaining that it was all Hitler but not them. I thought it was pretty awful. I'd had enough. I went as far as Cologne and I didn't want to go on. I could have gone back and worked in Fleet Street, but I'd been there before, so I thought I'd go home.

The situation for women journalists during the war was just like *Rosie the Riveter*, the film which showed how women did everything during the war. Everybody from the *Ladies' Home Journal* was a war correspondent for a short time. They would get an okay from the War Office, get the uniform and the typhoid shots and they'd turn up in Paris. The Americans sent everybody. There were women everywhere. Martha Gellhorn, the American writer, was up with the Ninth Airforce. She used to come swanning down to Paris for a bit of leave, dressed in uniform, parachute silk cravat, a mink coat and cowboy boots, then pop over to London to her favourite hairdresser. The women journalists ran as many risks as anybody else if they wanted to. Ernest Hemingway was there working for *Esquire*. His girlfriend, Lady Welsh, was there working for the London *Daily Express*. There were a lot of Australians there and you could just do a special article and they'd take back your accreditation, because accommodation was limited. But after the war, they pushed women back to the *status quo*. The same thing happened to the male journalists who went to Vietnam. They came back and had to cover the police courts or petty sessions. That never happened to me though, not only because I was very good, but because I always had good bosses, like Ezra Norton.

When I returned to Australia, Blue had a lamp burning in the window for me, but only just. Three years was a long time to be apart. We both worked in the day time, and behaved like an ordinary married couple. We were inclined just to stick around with ourselves. We had about three sets of friends – my friends, his friends and our friends. We had a very happy life because we both spent a lot of time on our own. We never spoke to each other at meals, we used to read. We led independent lives and we never questioned each other about what we were doing. I don't know how it worked, but it did. Oh I'm sure we were jealous, sexually and domestically, but it very seldom surfaced, and we were never jealous of each other as journalists.

On the domestic scene we both cooked. We shared the money and didn't care who paid for what. He would bring home beautiful things to eat and I would pay for a bottle of whisky. On the whole, I decided what was to happen in the house, but if we were invited somewhere, I would never accept without his okay. I didn't run our social life at all. If I was asked to do something, I would do it without reference to him. He had a whole life apart from me, because he did things I didn't – like going to the races. People would ring up and ask, 'Do you want to come or just Blue?' and I'd say, 'Oh, I don't want to come.' So that was all right. We would do the garden together. He'd do the harder work because I have a bad back. We'd go swimming together in the mornings at Bondi. Then he would say, 'I'm going in early, I don't like as much sun as you.' Maybe I'd get a bus or taxi back and he'd take the car. We didn't fight. He would simply have left me if there'd been rows. I knew that. I didn't nag. If I had something important to say I said it. I was often quite surprised that he didn't challenge me, and if he did challenge me I knew I should shut up or he would leave. He thought the same about me. We never did leave each other, you know. We never separated over a row.

I once asked Blue, 'Would you like to have a little boy running around the house . . .?' He said, 'No, thank you.' And that was that! He was self-sufficient and so was I.

At one stage I had a terrible pain in my insides and I didn't know what it was. I also thought I was pregnant. I had been pregnant twice before but lost each baby quite quickly. An obstetrician examined me and said, 'You've got fibroids.' I said, 'Yes, I'm pregnant too,' and he said, 'No, you're not.' I said, 'Well, we'll see.' He put me into hospital and I had a hysterectomy. He came to see me afterwards and told me it had been a successful operation and I had lost the baby. I said, 'There, I told you,' and I burst into floods of tears. He said, 'What are you crying for?' and I said, 'Because I can't have a baby.' And he said, 'You were never meant to have one, there's no need for you to cry.' Talk about bedside manner! But of course I wasn't meant to have a baby. I'd have had one, or asked why I couldn't have one, much earlier. I once asked Blue, 'Would you like to have a little boy running round the house in your old rugby colours?' He said, 'No thank you.' And that was that! He was self-sufficient and so was I.

After the airforce Blue took a dislike to journalism and he tried to buy a boat to go prawning or something. But he found that this was really an expert professional game, so he returned to journalism. He became news editor of a Sunday paper, but his heart was never in it. While I was committed to being a journalist for ever, he saw what was wrong with journalism, even then when it was a more honest profession. Now it's a lie. I don't see how you can be an honest journalist now. A few people manage it. Most journalists today don't really care if the truth gets into the paper or not. To them it's just a story. It absolutely horrifies me. I'm sure there are a few committed ones, but they're really up against it. Blue got out of journalism and for ten years he was the public relations officer for the Australian Wine Board. He was brilliant at it. He loved all the wine men, and worked as little as possible. I never saw a man arrange his life so well. He didn't care about money in the least; he spent what he had.

When he died in 1964 I had to take his cheque books and things to what he used to laughingly call his 'man of affairs', but they were incomprehensible. He didn't know a thing. He had some shares because he had friends who were stock brokers. He lived a Regency life and just had a good time. I was terribly worried about money when he died. I said to myself, 'How am I going to live?' I even cancelled his subscription to the *New Yorker*! I thought I couldn't afford it. I was absolutely irrational. I earned more money than he did. I took the *New Yorker* on again the next year as I couldn't live without it. I went into a terrible spin when he died. I cried all the time. I blamed him for leaving me. I couldn't stand it. And yet, I should be entirely honest, even in the early days of our marriage before I went away to the war, I had twice been blindly and hopelessly in love. I knew that he had had two love affairs, but they were never discussed. I'd never have left him, but I did wildly indiscreet things like rushing down to Melbourne to see this man off when he was having his sabbatical. So we both lied. I think the worst thing anybody can do to someone you love is to confess all, because I did love him more than anybody in the world. Telling all is a terrible thing to do to people. Thank God he never told me everything about himself. He was such a marvellous friend and he never bored me. I don't think I bored him either. We really suited each other down to the ground. That's worse when somebody like that dies. Even two years afterwards I would see something and I'd say to myself, 'Oh, I must tell Blue about that.' I've never got over him.

I'd had an operation for lung cancer a couple of years before Blue died. I didn't have chemotherapy or anything. It was a clean thing. It wasn't in my armpits or anywhere else. Of course it could come and attack me any day. I went into hospital not knowing what would happen to me until a couple of days later, after the operation. I was told by friends that he was distraught. But he never said anything about that to me. He just said, 'Well, now you're home.' But when he died, I was totally done for. You'd think I'd never had a separate life from him. I never wrote a poem after he died, not until 1979. In fact I did write two poems on the subject of bereavement. I was so bereft. They were published in the *Bulletin* and they were the last. I never wrote another one until 1979. I filled my life with rubbish. I didn't want to think about what had happened to me. I went to places I didn't want to go and saw people I didn't want to see, just so I wouldn't have to think. I went away a good bit. I even put Edward, his dog, in a home and went away. I couldn't bear to put Edward in a kennel . . . but I did. Eventually I did pull myself together.

When Blue was dying, my editor, Zel Rabin, and the GP used to come every night to see me. Blue had a stroke and it took him ten days to die. Of course he didn't want to live. He'd made sure that both the doctor and I knew that he was not to stay alive, because he wouldn't have to put up with anything like that. Having a cold for him was enough. We'd sit and drink whisky or brandy and we'd cry. The GP would cry and say, 'He's going to perish, darling, he's going to perish.' I'd say, 'Yes, but how long is he going to know that he's going to die?' 'Oh, he doesn't know anything,' Zel used to cry. Then two days after Blue died, Zel rang me and said, 'Come on, you're coming into work,' I said, 'No, no, I can't. I've got too many things to do.' He said, 'You are coming into work.' The next thing he did was to send me down to a mine tragedy. He wanted three pieces on it. I said, 'No, Zel, I can't go down to Bulli. I can't leave Edward anywhere.' He said, to coin his own words, 'Put fucking Edward in the car and go to Bulli and stay in a motel.' So I put fucking Edward in the car and the motel wouldn't take him. He had to sleep in the car and I had to sneak him in. I didn't know then, but Zel found out a few days later that he was riddled with cancer. He was thirty-six. Zel got me back to work. Then he died. I loved him. He left so many people bereaved. Then I just went back to work and stayed in the house a lot.

I was working at the *Daily Mirror* which had begun to go bad. When Zel died Rupert Murdoch turned it into a girlie afternoon paper. Zel had been able to stop him, but nobody else could. It became a most disgusting paper. He set me up with a little group of people of my own like the London *Sunday Times*. Nothing is ever innovative in Australia, it's all taken from some American or London paper or magazine. We were supposed to thoroughly investigate the education system for example. It was dreadful. I was rescued from there by Adrian Deamer, editor of the *Australian*. He could see what was happening to me and said, 'I'll ask Rupert if you can come on to the *Australian*.' Rupert used to keep such a personal eye on us. When he bought the *Mirror*, he was just a man who was in there all day running the paper. He was marvellous at it. He knew us all, loved us all, and he took our advice. When he made mistakes he got rid of them fast. When the *Australian* moved from Canberra to Sydney and I went on to it, he was always in the news-room. He could always be talked to and argued with. Now it's all gone bad. Why? Power! Power, not money.

I wasn't really aware that women in Australia were given a hard time in journalism. I was the one who was sent on the big stories, and given the bylines.

When I was on the *Australian* Adrian, a wonderful editor, sent me out on various jobs, like investigating the brewery network in Australia. Going round the country talking to people who run the enormously influential breweries, was one of the most fascinating things I've ever done. I won a Walkely award for that. Then I did a series of quite big jobs for the *Australian*. Now and again he'd give me something I didn't want to do or didn't understand, like, 'Tell me what's happening at TAA.' He forced me to do it.

I wasn't really aware that women in Australia were given a hard time in journalism. I was the one who was sent on the big stories, and given the bylines. The famous Eric Baume was my editor once on the *Daily Guardian*. He sent me to do the most appalling things. One night he sent me out after the races to cover an accident in which three jockeys had been killed. I was out there with a photographer and bits of jockeys lying around. It was a big Saturday night/Sunday morning story because of racing. People were going along picking up fragments of jockeys. I had to do everything. There were no other women on the paper. Most of the other women journalists were on the social pages, but they were no particular friends of mine. Connie Robinson of the *Herald* could have done any job they'd given her. She proved that when she was sent to England after the war to write about rationing and clothes and things. She sent back the most splendid stuff about the state of the country and how it was run. But on the whole the other women didn't get any good stories to do. They were given the rotten stories.

The only time I knew I was being badly treated by my colleagues was in Fleet Street. But they were also treating me badly because I was Australian.

Up until I left the *Australian*, which was a couple of years ago, the editor did not come in on Sunday. It's said to be a day of no news – nothing happens in Australia on a Sunday. So they put an acting news editor on the news-desk. It would be the cadet, or the copy boy rather than the most experienced woman on the staff. At least on the *Herald* they had a woman foreign editor, Margaret Jones. They haven't had a woman news editor; they don't in Fleet Street either. Fleet Street is tougher with women than anywhere. Adrian Deamer was totally in favour of women. He took an interest in what they did, and would let them do politics or anything. Once I did politics for the *Sunday Telegraph* when Cyril Pearl was the editor. I used to go up to Canberra from Tuesday to Friday and come back to write it up. Then I was the lead interviewer and critic for the Arts pages in the *Australian*. When I eventually retired I was taken back the next day as the editor of the book pages. I ran that entirely to suit myself and Rupert Murdoch never interfered with my television reviewing or the book pages.

I didn't want to be an editor. I once edited a women's

magazine for a year and I nearly killed it. It just died. They were most relieved when I said I couldn't do it. I had no idea what to put in it. I've always been a consultant editor, but I've never sat in the editorial chair. I certainly never wanted to. It's a hot seat. It's the one you get fired from. They get tired of you if the circulation doesn't keep going up. Australia is littered with ex-editors of the *Australian.* I wouldn't want that.

While I was on the *Australian* I had a terrible car accident. I asked Rupert if I could go and work in London for a while. I've always been addicted to England. I worked in the bureau there for two years and that's when the women's movement was going full blast. I came back to find it here. I'm totally sympathetic to it, but I've never felt that I knew anything about it, because I missed the bus. They were women in their thirties and it was important to them. But you can see that it never affected my life. Now there were a few people like me who did what they wanted. For instance, Beatrice Davis, an editor with Angus & Robertson Publishers (A & R), brought to Australia and edited all the good writers for thirty years. She didn't know that she was different either. The only time I knew that I was being badly treated by my colleagues was in Fleet Street. But they were also treating me badly because I was Australian. Women there get a bad time still. I don't know about America. One of the things about journalism is that we've never been paid less. Equal pay makes a lot of difference to your attitude. In so many professions or trades you don't get the same money.

I read Germaine Greer just because she was interesting. I've always read Doris Lessing. I can't read Simone de Beauvoir. I don't know why, but there are always authors you can't read. I find her schoolmistressy. I can't stand preachers, male or female. I do not want to be addressed by anybody. Maybe that's why the women's movement hasn't reached the working class women. They're much harder to get at of course. They need it and yet they seem to adore their washing-machine life. I mean they're so house-proud. Middle class women are slommicking around in dressing-gowns talking about the women's movement till two o'clock in the afternoon, having a good time. Working class women have everything spick and span.

Angus & Robertson published my first book of poems in 1954. I don't have a favourite poem. I like them as I write them. Now

I've nothing to lose. I'm trying to write totally what I mean. When I was younger I was very addicted to the beautiful phrase. Now I'm ruthless with it. If it doesn't mean exactly what I say then out it goes. Once, on a ship coming back from England, I wrote a novel. There was nothing else to do. I entered it in a competition in New Zealand and it wasn't even highly recommended. It's such a good thing that nobody published it. It was really appalling. It's long gone of course, but it would have been awful if I'd been saddled with that all my life. My terrible poetry has disappeared too. It was never collected, so I can't be blamed for that. But you do silly things when you're young.

Two of my writer friends, Douglas Stewart and Patrick White, would tell you that I'm always writing about death. Even though I'm a cheerful person, intellectually I'm a pessimist. I know it's going to end badly, but in practice I'm quite optimistic. I think, 'Today's going to be all right.' I don't think that when I go to bed, but I think that when I wake up in the morning. Transience is what it's all about. I had one poem in the *Overland* recently and Patrick said, 'There you go again,' because he sighted it. They call it death. I think it's transience. It's rage against it. When Blue died I thought, 'How dare he go off and leave me.' But that's what makes everything so good – that it's not going to last. Secretly, I think I'm going to be the only one that doesn't die. I'm going to live forever.

Now I'm writing what I'll call *Observations*. Richard Walsh, A&R's publisher, says that is the most unsaleable title in the whole world, but he's got the rights to the book. I'm a great friend of author David Malouf and when I was staying with him in Italy recently he decided that I should write the things that I'd found out about life. While I was there that Christmas, when there were only Italians around, I had that curious feeling of remoteness from the world. I decided that I might write about some of my thoughts rather than chronological memoirs. David said to Richie, 'Betty is going to write about her life.' So Richie took me to a big lunch somewhere and said, 'Can I have the first refusal?' I said, 'Of course you can.' But I don't think I'm going to do it. Last night I saw him and he said, 'Have you done anything?' I've actually done 12 000 words, but it doesn't matter if it's never done because there are too many books anyway. There's Clive James' memoirs and Martin Johnston was trying to write the life of George and Charmian Johnston. Who needs mine? I don't know if I've turned up in any of Patrick's books yet – thinly disguised as a cook! Perhaps the next novel.

I'm not very creative because my whole life has been semi-creative. As a journalist, some of your creative juice is gone by the end of the day. You feel like sitting down, as I've done all my life, just reading. I know some quite good writers who say, 'I would rather read than write.' I agree with them. Look at the books I haven't read yet. Very few peole can stand collections of their journalism. I've just reviewed Fay Weldon's book, *Watching Me Watching You*. All the stories were done for various magazines. The collection is not nearly as good as her novels where she sat down with a theme and wound it out of her navel.

My hates? I hate poor English. I hate people who use sociological language. I hate words like 'supportive' and 'parameters'. I hate that more than I hate advertising jargon. I stand up and stamp when that happens. I don't hate anything else much.

My loves? Love. That's all. I remember being interviewed against my will by a very clever man. He asked me what I loved. I said simply, 'Love'. I heard it later on the radio. It sounded so sensual.

Journalists are notorious and glorious gossips. The interview was punctuated with tantalising asides like, 'Turn the tape off and I'll tell you the real story.'

What seemed like, and in fact was, many hours later, I staggered up the steps into the street. I felt quite drunk with the details of a life so overflowing: a life that spanned so many countries and people; a life so full of first-hand knowledge of events; and an analysis of it all that made it as clear and sharp as the light of the Sydney summer afternoon into which I was driving.

EVE MAHLAB (Businesswoman and lawyer)

I sank into the soft cushions of the chair and waited for Eve to finish with a client. The modern, well-organised office hummed with the quiet efficiency of women working together. My eyes lit upon the painting on the wall opposite me – an original John Olsen.

Before I could really indulge my envy, Eve ushered me into her office offering cheese and biscuits left over from lunch. She explained how her husband had brought them when he had popped in to see her as a surprise. Not too many husbands do that after twenty-odd years of marriage. Lucky lady, I thought to myself.

'Well, let's get started,' she said, with an aura of calm, cool confidence.

My earliest memories are feelings of fear and apprehension. I was born in Vienna in 1937, just before the Nazis came in. My parents lost their home and their business in the first few years of my life. We were hidden in a hotel. Mother's father was in a concentration camp and my father was in a depot prior to being sent to a camp. My mother managed to get them out. She was heroic. However, for years after, every time my mother went out, I thought she wouldn't come back. I've also been left with this tremendous feeling of opposition to oppression. Now, when I'm fighting men, I sometimes wonder whether I'm just replacing one set of oppressors with another.

We were refugees. There weren't many migrants in Australia at that time. When I was two I was sent to school to learn English. I could only speak German, which was a pretty unpopular language. I went to the Loreto Convent. I remember a nun hoisting me over the back fence as my mother left me to go to work. I was very happy there. Then we moved out to East Malvern to a large, run-down old house in what then was almost a country atmosphere. We were terribly well treated there because we were oddities in the community even though, as enemy aliens, my father had to report regularly at the police station and we weren't allowed to have cameras or anything like that.

I knew there was something different about us and that my parents spoke in a funny way. I very much resented my mother not coming to school mothers' clubs. It was only when I got older that I realised that she was very aware of her difference. She felt she was doing me a disservice by participating in a fairly conservative mothers' club.

My parents developed a manufacturing business. During the war dolls were not imported into Australia, so they hired some staff and started making dolls in sheds behind the house, and I grew up in a family where my mother and father and several other caring adults were present. I'm not conscious of one parent having had more of an influence on me than the other. All I know is that they were both there. I always had a tremendously close relationship with my father. I was an only child. It might have been different if he'd had a son, but as it was, he placed all his care and concern in me. So I had two good models: my father working at home and my mother actively enjoying the business. In later years she said it was the happiest time in her life. My parents worked very hard. No one got up in the morning to make me breakfast. I made it myself, and I went to school by myself. I just took it for granted that I had to do things for myself and be independent. At that stage I didn't resent it at all. Although as I got older and more conservative, I began to think, 'Why can't they be like other people's parents?' Now it's gone full circle and I'm glad that they weren't.

My parents worked very hard . . . I just took it for granted that I had to do things for myself and be independent.

When I was ten, my parents decided to join my mother's

parents in New York. As you can imagine, we had left Europe in very pressing circumstances and her parents had not been able to come to Australia. They'd gone to New York and she missed them greatly during the War. We lived there for a year but we were all so miserable that we came back to Australia. For a short time I went to Korowa Girls' School but I was very unhappy there. I was really a social outcast. I had a small group of three or four friends but the majority of girls hated me and the teachers considered me a trouble-maker. I was very bright and I did extremely well in every subject, except art. When this brought my average down at the end of the year I felt that most of the girls and the teachers were terribly pleased. I can laugh now, but I was just so unhappy at the time. I left Korowa after some atrocious rows both with the staff and the girls. A lot of my trouble stemmed from my non-conformist approach. The others were just so conventional and many of them were very petty in their attitudes. For many years I blamed myself. Then I realised that there was something wrong with *them*. I was all right. I ultimately left and went to Methodist Ladies' College where the girls were better but the staff were even more repressive, but at least it was 'career oriented'.

I didn't compromise any of my activities because there was a man in my life who didn't like it, or who I had to give time to.

I knew I was going to be a lawyer, because my father told me. He had one philosophy that he repeated to me over the years: that I was very difficult, very outspoken, very independent and would never find a man to put up with me. I would therefore have to be able to support myself. Because I talked a lot and was very articulate, law was the obvious choice, but it also had a lot to do with their thwarted ambitions. As middle class Europeans who had lost everything and come out here as second-rate citizens, they wanted to regain for me what they had lost in status and position. There was always a strong pressure on me and I always tried very hard, not just for myself, but to please them. Sometimes I came second in class and my father would say, 'That's great, who came first?' Finally, though I did very well academically, I wasn't allowed to go to the speech night because I told a teacher off in the last week at school.

Then I got to university and I loved it. In the Jewish community girls marry early and many of my girlfriends were dropping out of university because it didn't really matter. My parents were absolutely supportive and adamant that I finish my studies. We used to laugh because I didn't have many steady boyfriends. I had a variety and whenever a young man came to the house for the second time, my mother would say in the royal plural, 'You realise we do not go steady in this house.' It got to be a joke. There were absolutely no pressures on me to marry. It didn't even occur to me. I did have an infatuation with one guy who didn't care for me, and that rather saved me from any other serious entanglements. I didn't compromise any of my activities because there was a man in my life who didn't like it, or who I had to give time to. I just had a ball. I finished university a year early. The carrot that had always been dangled in front of my nose was an overseas trip when I finished university.

When I came back, I didn't know what had hit me, because my parents had changed. I was twenty-one, and suddenly every young man was considered to be a marriage prospect. It was almost Jekyll and Hyde. I started fighting with my parents. I ran away from home to Sydney and met Frank, my husband. We decided to marry about a week after we met. I was physically very attracted to him. I have this theory that you tend to fall in love when the conditions are right. The fact that I was at that time of life and the pressures were on, just suddenly made him very attractive. Probably if I'd met him five years earlier, he wouldn't even have taken a tumble. Anyway, he turned me on, and not all that many guys did. I was afraid to tell my mother that he was American as she had always been separated from her parents. He came down from Sydney before I got up the courage to tell my parents. When I did, all hell broke loose. My mother virtually didn't speak to me for some time but my father was more encouraging and they finally came around. In the end, my mother adored him and by the time we got married, it was with their approval. Everyone's amazed that I'm still married, including myself. That's one of my achievements – and my husband's!

I'd done my articles in Melbourne with a matrimonial firm, but when I went to Sydney I worked for the Public Solicitor. They virtually carried me out of there when I was pregnant. This guy came in and wanted to take proceedings against a dentist because a cavity had become gangrenous. The gory details

My husband had always said to me, 'You can work, so long as the children and I don't suffer.' Eventually I said, '. . . you and the children might suffer . . . but that's too bad.'

were too much for me. I passed out. They carried me home and wouldn't let me come back again. At that time my husband was close to finishing his three-year contract as a senior executive for a large American corporation. When we looked at the prospect of going back to a small town in the United States, we didn't want that. My father had a business here in Melbourne, but no son to take it on, and a daughter who was completely uninterested at that stage, so he made an offer to my husband, who accepted. We came to live in Melbourne and that was another unhappy time. My husband didn't get on with my father in business. There were all sorts of conflicts. I think they were actually fighting over me. But as soon as our daughter was born that changed and my father shifted his affections to my daughter. I don't understand what the mechanics of it all were. Ultimately they decided that they were going to sell the business anyway. My husband then moved into other areas and from then on, they got on terribly well. I continued to have trouble with my mother. I still haven't worked out why that was, but there always has been a lot of fighting between my mother and I.

After I had my daughter, I didn't work. I was gradually going round the bend. I had three children in three-and-a-half years. I made that choice because I have always wanted to do what you were 'meant' to do better than anyone else. But somehow I didn't develop any independent critical thought. All the newspapers were talking about childcare and maternal deprivation and that good mothers stayed with their children all the time. My parents said, 'You idiot, you've got this law degree and you should be out working. You are not the sort of person to stay at home with children.' I told them it was none of their business.

Although I was at home, I still had some household help, and I can remember reading one of these articles and realising I was out of the house an awful lot because of this household help. I said to myself, 'I'm not being a good mother.' So I got rid of the household help and did everything myself. In the next year I put on a stone and a half in weight. One day I hit one of my children terribly, terribly hard, and took her off to a psychiatrist because she was so difficult. The psychiatrist said, 'Mrs Mahlab, there's nothing wrong with the child, but there's something wrong with you. Why don't you go back to work?' So I did. Those three years at home were the unhappiest years of my life. I was a bad mother and should have listened to my parents because they could see it was wrong for me and it wasn't too good for the children either. My husband had always said to me, 'You can work, so long as the children and I don't suffer.' Eventually I said, 'Well, look, you and the children might suffer if I go back to work, but that's too bad. I'm going to do it anyway.'

He never actively tried to stop me doing anything. He has been supportive – well, at least non-committal – in many of the areas that I have chosen to move into. There's only been one situation where he's come down hard. I did exactly the thing he didn't want me to do. We were house-hunting, and I saw a house which I liked a lot. He not only disliked it, he wouldn't discuss it. Sort of, 'This is my word, I will not discuss it any further.' I had some Broken Hill Proprietary (BHP) shares which my grandfather had left me. I thought, 'To hell with you. I'm going to buy this house by myself, and I'm going to sell these shares for a deposit.' So I went out and sold the shares. It was the day before BHP discovered gas in Bass Strait and the shares either doubled or tripled! It's still one of those not-so-funny jokes. Of course I didn't buy the house – a house is for two people. But it was the authoritarian attitude I reacted to. My father told my husband that he'd have to realise that I was terribly difficult and that he just couldn't treat me in the traditional way. He cottoned on to that and he hasn't acted in an authoritarian way to me since.

If I had it over again, I'd put them in childcare from the earliest moment . . . It's the mother's guilt that affects children, not the childcare.

I started looking for work. People just laughed at me. Part time work for lawyers was unheard of at that time. Eventually a friend helped me get a job for one day a week. After I started, lots of firms rang me back and said they were interested in taking me on. I thought to myself, 'There should be some kind of agency that places married women lawyers who want part time employment.' I filed it away in the back of my mind and went off to my part time job. After about a year I realised I was getting all the shit work because if you are only in the office one day a week, you can't do ongoing work. But again I had to get terribly depressed before I really faced up to the fact that I wasn't being challenged.

I resigned from work and started looking around for something to do. I went back to this idea of an agency for women who were looking for locum work as lawyers. I wrote a letter to every law firm in Melbourne stating my experience and the fact that I was particularly qualified to evaluate staff for them. In the first week I made two placements and these funded the advertising and promotion of the firm. Working from home I developed my consultancy which recruited lawyers for law firms in Melbourne. One of the justifications for starting it from home was that I could be with the kids at the same time as working. As it got busier it became quite clear that this was an absolute myth. The phone was always ringing. I wasn't doing my work properly and I wasn't doing my mothering properly because my mind was always split. So I knocked on all the doors in St Kilda Road until I found an office.

As soon as I moved the overheads went up. I thought, 'If this agency works for lawyers, it will work for some other group.' So I employed a married woman accountant to recruit accountants and a married women architect to recruit architects. The accountants were just indifferent but the architects did very well. We expanded virtually overnight. The following year I was enjoying it so much I decided that if it worked in Melbourne, it would work in Sydney. I opened an office there and it did work, although we never got the architectural side off the ground there. My partner was a sole parent and it was much harder for her to travel. She didn't have the support of a husband as I did, and so for many years the Sydney business wasn't as viable as the one down here.

One of the traits of the recruitment business is that it goes up and down in response to economic developments, recessions, and so on, so I started looking around for a way to expand. By this time I was getting sick of working very, very hard. Interviewing lawyers is a very mentally demanding task. I set down a list of things I was looking for. Firstly, whatever I took on had to be less labour intensive for me personally, and secondly, it had to be immune from economic recession in so far as was possible.

I decided to publish diaries. Once you publish a diary, in

theory you can go on publishing it from year to year. People tend to get hooked on diaries. Once they've used one, they want the same format every year. I first published a diary for lawyers that I'd seen somewhere else. We've since expanded into diaries for accountants and diaries for builders. They've filled the gap that I wanted to fill. We also do costing for solicitors and when we started this, I saw it as a marvellous opportunity to employ solicitors who were married women, who were exceptionally able, and who were available to do this work because they wanted to work at home. Often it was the most important thing to them, both from a financial and from a work satisfaction point of view. Some women have come here and lasted two days, but those here now show no signs of going even though one has grown beyond her work. I have no way to expand it for her.

We do other things for our staff like financing them into buying property, as men do for their executives. Most of them are separated and they're not going to the discos any more looking for guys. They've got their little properties and they're really quite happy. They'd like guys and companionship but they don't necessarily want to get married. I've always said to them, 'If you have your own property your relationship with the man you meet is different than if he thinks you're going to be dependent on him.' It's been so in my marriage and I promote that to other women. If any of the staff have a crisis I become involved because it gets to me one way or another. Then I hold their hands. When things are coasting along well, I don't. I don't know who has a boyfriend, or what his name is. Perhaps I should, but I don't. Half the time I'm in a haze. I tend to be very single-minded. But if they have to make a major decision, particularly on anything that's financial or terribly emotional, then I'm involved – at least, with most of them. One of them tends to be very quiet and a bit of a loner, and our relationship is mainly cerebral. She's a feminist and she cuts out newspaper articles all the time and we discuss them. Another comes from a very traditional Catholic background and all the things that she's been angry about all her life now have a place in the philosophy. She's blossomed tremendously.

Looking back, the roles of mother and worker co-existed terribly well. We knew I was going to work, so we looked for a house that had a granny flat. We employed a couple to live in this flat so that at night the door between the flat and the house was open and they could babysit. Over the years, we had a series of lovely couples who were like grandparents to the children. That lifted a lot of pressure from me. In the beginning I thought I had to do this domestic work, but I grew out of that. I saw no tremendous value in doing housework and I spent my spare time with the children. I still cooked the meals at night because that's the time when they're sitting around and you're doing things together. Over those years I was racked with guilt like all mothers who worked at that time. Quite wrongly. If I had it over again, I'd put them in childcare from the earliest moment. I see young women who work for me now doing that without any ill effects whatsoever. It's the mother's guilt that affects children, not the childcare. The kids have always accepted it. They've never been resentful about it. In fact, Frank once asked them, 'Do you think you were neglected?' and they said, 'No.' Maybe they were just trying to be nice. But I look at them and even if they were neglected they are functioning so well. They're autonomous individuals at a fairly early age and doing well in what they've chosen to do. I have a lovely relationship with them. They've all had the opportunity to move out and to go overseas.

I had an independent business. I structured my own time . . . I could practically always decide whether I was going to work in the middle of the night.

When I was reading about Germaine Greer and women's liberation in the early '70s, I was one of those women who said, 'But I am liberated,' and, 'What a lot of nonsense.' Then in the *Nation Review*, I saw an ad for the Women's Electoral Lobby (WEL) and I thought, 'Women? Politics? I'm really interested in all that.' It must have been the second or third meeting of WEL. It was in a little house in Carlton and Beatrice Faust was there. They were all young women academics. They needed someone to draft the constitution. I offered to draft it and from that time I was involved. That constitution was the funniest thing because a constitution is a structure for an organisation, but this was an organisation that didn't want a structure. I'm still confused about what the assignment really was and I can't imagine why I took it on. I just liked the group and I liked the excitement, and obviously, the more the principles infiltrated into my consciousness, the more I became committed to

women's liberation. As time went on, I got more and more involved. I'm not sure why it happened this way, but I was willing to take on the task of being an advocate. WEL didn't have any hierarchy and it didn't have any formal positions, but in fact I was the one who spoke to the press and to groups. I was the one who promoted the principles. Many of the women in WEL weren't willing to take that up-front position, for all kinds of reasons. Many of them were employed and thought their jobs would be placed on the line if they got involved with what was at that stage viewed as a radical organisation. Others had internalised those middle class attitudes like not showing off or looking for publicity, and that there was something unfeminine about speaking out. Whilst they supported what I was doing, they weren't willing to do it themselves. So, almost by default, just about every media appearance fell to me. I lost some business as a result of it but not too much. I was willing to take the risk.

In 1972 the first thing that WEL did, and it was in process before I joined, was to produce a questionnaire which they administered to every candidate in the 1972 Federal election. The candidates had to answer questions on women's issues and WEL had arranged with the *Age* to publish a form guide, rating each candidate. It was brilliant. I was astounded at the ability of these women to put together something like that. It went off terribly well. The following year, there was a State election and we had to do something. I suggested a public forum called, 'Why should women vote for you?' in which the leaders of the political parties fielding candidates in the 1973 State election would get on the platform and answer women's questions. Previously, politicians had said women vote the way their husbands vote. They had never even heard of childcare and were just so ignorant about the needs of women. We made issues of these things. I was chosen to chair the meeting and it was one of the most exciting times of my life. We had to struggle to get all the politicians there. Rosslyn Smallwood, a very active member of WEL, knew the director of the Liberal Party and through him arranged for the leader to attend. Armed with that, I then approached the leader of the Labor Party and said, 'Well, Dick Hamer's going to come, you'd better come.' He said, 'Well, if Hamer's going, I'll be there too.' And then we went to the Country Party. So we got the leader of the Country Party, the leader of the Liberal Party, the leader of the Labor Party and the leader of the DLP. That was a coup. I don't think the four leaders of the parties had ever appeared on the one platform. We hired the Dallas Brooks Hall which holds 2 500 people. We had to turn people away. One of the things that I was able to do that many of the others didn't have the skills for, was make money. We needed money desperately. It occurred to me that we should sell this forum to television, which we did for several thousand dollars. The programme was so interesting and so popular that it was replayed four days later. The effect on women was quite startling. The whole thing was incredibly controversial and the money kept WEL going for many years afterwards.

I stayed on for several years after that but then I got impatient because WEL has two functions which, in my opinion are almost incompatible. On the one hand it has this anti-elitism where if you do take a leading position, you do it by default. You don't have any formal position to sustain you or to give you authority. Really you're looking over your shoulder all the time because you don't have that. On the other hand it tries to be egalitarian and nurture new women coming into WEL to give them confidence, to let them participate in all sorts of decisions. After several years of sitting through these general meetings and re-inventing the wheel as new women entered the movement all the time, feeling that I had more to contribute because I had many years of experience, yet feeling guilty about talking out of turn in case I intimidated the 'tender young buds' opening up, it just got a little bit much. Because I'd been in it for so long I was getting terribly arrogant. My business had been going downhill because of my tremendous involvement, so I gradually withdrew.

The pressures on all our marriages were enormous. Frank was pretending to be supportive but was really under tremendous pressure. To have a wife taking on this women's lib. role made him the subject of an awful lot of public teasing – you know, who wears the pants? He coped with it very well. But basically, his heart was not in it. He supported me because that was what I wanted to do. He believes that individuals in a marriage should be free to be themselves. Although ideologically he's not a feminist, he acts like a feminist, whereas most men ideologically say they're feminists and want to promote women, in practice they're not. Their wives are usually in the traditional role, and with us it's just the opposite.

If people see you as an active feminist they think you put the family second . . . I've proved that's not true. Families have to adjust so that women aren't so oppressed within them.

As a result of my involvement in WEL, I'd been appointed to all sorts of 'respectable' things, like the Monash University Council, the Board of the Australian Institute of Political Science. The only trouble was, they just didn't turn me on. I found that outside the women's movement I really felt half-dead. I kept out for a couple of years, although they still used me in a consultant capacity. But I really didn't get heavily involved again until 1979. In the meantime, one of my very good friends gained the position of Co-ordinator of Women's Affairs in Victoria. Through her, I heard that there was to be a national conference in Canberra to develop an Australian Plan of Action for the second half of the United Nations Decade for Women. Delegates to the conference were to be elected by Victorian women interested enough to vote. There had been a whole series of preliminary meetings and I realised that the ultra-right – the 'Women who want to be Women' – looked as if they were going to control the conference. I saw this as a tremendous danger, because it would be seen as representing public opinion rather than a vocal minority group. I got in touch with WEL, who were thinking the same thoughts. WEL and women's liberation had a meeting, which brought together the whole spectrum of women's organisations, and worked out a ticket of fifteen people. The group ranged from the centre, where I see myself, all the way to the far left. A lot of them were very reasonable but there were a few of them that saw me as the right. I suppose to a certain extent I am to the right, but most of them could see that we needed a broad coalition to beat this ultra-conservative faction. We succeeded. 4 000 women registered to vote and we got 2 000 votes. We got eleven people on to the National Women's Advisory Council, and they passed some wonderful resolutions, although were immediately told these had no force at all as the government didn't think itself bound to follow them.

Nevertheless, I believe that was an important achievement for the women's movement. If we are going backwards at present we're going back a little slower than we would have been without it. I loved that whole experience because it brought me not only back into WEL but back into the women's movement generally. Following that I went to Copenhagen as one of WEL's representatives for the International Decade of Women United Nations Forum. In fact as far as the Liberal Party, in which I am quite active, is concerned I really am a bit of a dark horse. In WEL they consider me to be terribly conservative and in the Liberal Party they think I'm terribly radical. It's been my fate always to be an outsider; not quite to belong.

Do I consider myself a powerful woman? I've always had trouble with the concept of power because in a democracy there isn't absolute power anywhere. There are all these checks and balances. People are always saying, 'The media has too much power, big business has too much power, or unions have too much power.' Actually they're all balancing each other and jockeying for positions. What I do think is that women are *powerless*. Of all groups, women have really very little power and very little influence. I used to think that men had positions of paid power and women had positions of unpaid influence but, on the whole, the unpaid positions they have tend to be those that care for society's victims – the aged, the children, the disabled. When it comes to being part of governments, the number of women who have influence is absolutely infinitesimal. I suppose I'm amongst the few that do have it, but I don't have a lot. I can get a good hearing when I speak to people. I'm on various committees that make decisions so that I help by just being there and saying things like, 'How does this affect women? Does it affect them differently from men? Are you assuming that all families are traditional with the woman at home and, if so, shouldn't we question that?' If you can ask those questions at the time the decisions are made, rather than jumping up and down after they have been made, I think you can be influential. I used to have political aspirations. I stood for pre-selection three times. By the third time, I was spending too much time on it, and once again my business was suffering so I had to make a choice. The closer I got to it the less it interested me. I'm not tolerant enough. I had other alternatives which were more attractive to me.

The future? Probably more of the same. I spent a month in New York, a mid-life sabbatical, trying to reassess where I was going. But bombs didn't start exploding in my head. One of my problems is that ninety per cent of my time is involved in keeping my business standing and growing. I get very frustrated as

it doesn't leave me more time for new initiatives and new areas, yet it's too good to leave it. All I know is that in the second half of my life I will have less obligations. My children are older. I have more time. There will be opportunities and I will be able to take them. I'm just leaving myself open to them as they come. I haven't got any particular goal. There is a slight fear that if you have so much enjoyment and so much activity in the first half of your life, can you actually keep up the pace? Will the opportunities keep coming? Haven't you had more than your fair share of the 'goodies'? Are you going to pay in the second half just on the law of averages? That could happen, but it doesn't seem to be. The other fear is that I do have a lot of responsibilities in running a business. When I think of what we have to make every month just to break even, I wonder how I got myself in this position. But I am here and I have coped. When I look back and think of some of the things I did, I can't imagine how I ever had the nerve. I don't think I could do them again. But they were done, and I have faith that somehow the good things will keep happening. I jolly well hope so anyway.

My first advice to young women is to consider business, because very few do. My daughters are more interested in helping people and I can understand this as I was the same at their age. The idea of being a real estate agent or something in the private sector isn't seen as being terribly altruistic. They're more interested in work that has some social involvement, and so was I when I was a lawyer. But in the long term, being in business and more particularly, being self-employed is a marvellous thing for women. One of the reasons that I've had a fairly interesting life and that I was able to be useful to WEL was that I had an independent business. I structured my own time. Sure, I had to work very hard at times, but I could practically always decide whether I was going to work in the middle of the night, whereas most of my contemporaries had nine-to-five jobs. Not only that, because I was in business, it was the market that decided whether I was doing a good job or not and whether people would pay for what I was doing, whereas so many of my friends were frustrated because some superior, often a man, made judgements on their performance which were absolutely unrelated to their performance but were to do with his prejudices. I saw many of them just wither up from frustration. To me, being self-employed has these advantages. It's particularly good because both in theory and in practice there is more of a chance of combining self-employment with a family life. You can structure the two things around each other. A lot of women are put off business by this feminine notion that somehow it's a bit unfeminine to think about money and success. That's a myth. I would like to see more women consider business and develop financial and managerial skills. It's potentially a good way to spend your life. There's more chance in business. Most of the opportunities are in the private sector.

There is an area of me that's very private and I am very committed to my family. If I don't see my children regularly and know what they're doing I feel terribly deprived. I value tremendously my relationship with my husband, which is a good one. We're really good friends. If people see you as being an active feminist they think that you put the family second or that liberation has to be at the expense of the family. I think I've proved that's not true. Families have to adjust so that women aren't so oppressed within them. My family has adjusted to consider my needs as important. I'm not just here to look after them. However, outwardly my life has been terribly traditional. I am still married to the same man. I have three children. I wear traditional clothes. Although I advocate change, and I believe society has to change, I have pretty much lived by the conventional, middle class, bourgeois rules.

I believe in change and I believe in reform. Whilst the system is as it is, I'll live pretty much within it and hope to change it from the inside. I'll use whatever privileges I have to make it better for other women. I'll continue to fight so that other women can have the same choices as I have. There must be more choices. On the other hand women need to learn to live with the uncertainty that having choices brings with it.

It was hard not to feel envious of a woman like Eve who really has managed to have her cake and eat it too. A successful business of her own, a happy marriage, a good relationship with her independent kids and a commitment to other women and their struggle.

'Is there anything else you want to achieve?'

'Yes, I would like to be Businesswoman of the Year.'

'Surely it's in the bag.'

'Not necessarily.'

It was five-thirty and the rush hour. At Eve's suggestion we boarded a tram in St Kilda Road. We continued to talk about women and success whilst clinging to the straps above our heads. 'Here's your stop,' she said. I clambered off, waved, and watched the tram rattle off into the misty Melbourne twilight.

A few months later I saw her on the front cover of the *Bulletin* – she had won the Qantas Businesswoman of the Year Award.

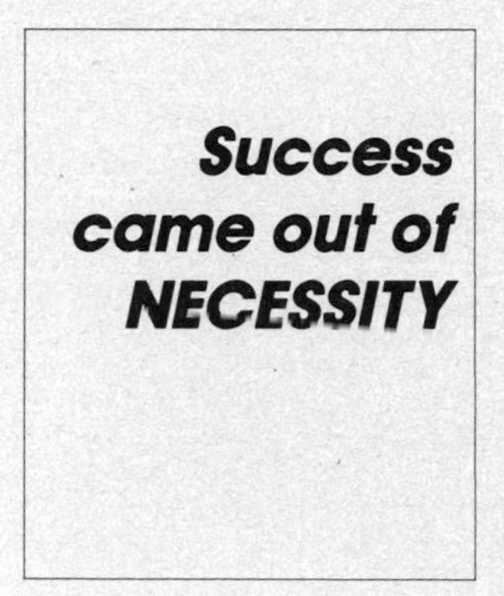
Success
came out of
NECESSITY

Outside events and, to some degree, other people dictated the necessity for these women to have a strong self-image. They felt that they had to put themselves first and believe in themselves or they, and those dependent on them, would never have survived. Having gained a sense of their own strength, they never looked back. Once a woman becomes the subject in her own life, she is on the path to success.

Mima Stojanovic desperately wanted to be a doctor but the untimely death of her father prevented her from studying medicine. Disappointed but not defeated she chose geology instead. When she was only twenty-nine, her husband died. She was forced to pull herself together and establish herself as a success in her profession. Her entire family was dependent on her for physical survival. She came through this crisis knowing nothing would ever defeat her again.

Robyn Nevin had an extremely tense and unhappy childhood. Her parents' break-up forced her to create a fantasy world of her own in order to survive the turmoil. The collapse of her own marriage meant that she alone was in control. She had a child to support. She knows the importance of keeping a strong sense of self and a belief in your own ability, especially in the acting profession. Never compromising this is the key to her success.

Joy Baluch began her life with a very poor self-image. Her marriage to a migrant and his inability to cope with the prejudice and discrimination he met, forced her to take control. It also taught her to fight. She took up cause after cause and won. Even though most recently she has experienced a couple of losses, her belief in herself remains undaunted.

MIMA STOJANOVIC (Geologist)

When I was introduced to Mima I shook her hand. She said, 'Are you Australian?' I said, 'Yes, why?' She said, 'In Australia when I meet somebody for the first time I never know where to put my hand. It's incredible that only men in Australia shake hands. Why are Australian women afraid to be warm?'

Nobody, not even the most inhibited Australian, could fail to respond with warmth to Mima. Her territory is the Adelaide University Museum where she lovingly attends to her thousands of rocks. She introduced me to a few of her favourites. Face aglow she explained to me why geology was such an exciting profession. I'll never treat a rock in the same way again.

I was born in Šabac which is a town with about 50 000 inhabitants about eighty kilometres from Belgrade. My mother was a housewife, and she enjoyed her motherhood and had a very hospitable open house. My father was a high school teacher who spoke beautiful French as a lot of Russian migrants did. He insisted that I go to French school at the age of five. In Yugoslavia we start primary school at seven so we don't matriculate until the age of nineteen. That has never changed because we think that deciding about your future at the age of seventeen is too early. I always wanted to study medicine. I think I really could be a very good doctor. In my country there is no such a thing as being a nurse because you are a woman. I was born free and all my generation was born free. In Yugoslavia, especially after the war when the women were fighting alongside the men, no one made a distinction between men and women. My parents used to have a relaxation period after lunch every day. We were condemned to silence. Usually we quietly played doctor and nurses. Once I had a big needle and I gave injections to my sister who screamed. My father jumped from their bedroom. Not only had my sister got the needle but she got a slap from him as well. It wasn't her fault at all, it was all mine. That was my first and last experience of being a doctor. My dream was not to be!

My father influenced me very much. He wanted me to be a person who was open for friendship and open-minded. He insisted I should speak at least three languages and follow different cultures. In his opinion that was the most important thing. Being able to understand another culture automatically means you understand the people. I was fifteen when he disappeared. He was assumed to be against communism because he was a Russian migrant. It was 1944 and the time of the revolution. People just disappeared, very often without trial.

The second influence was my professor, a very old Russian professor who was an immigrant in Yugoslavia. He encouraged me a lot. I was always an excellent student. So were my younger brother and sister. For many reasons, mostly political, I was not allowed to study medicine. It was only for certain people. But you could apply for the other disciplines. I was absolutely shattered because I simply didn't know that something else could exist for me. Then I went to university and the smallest queue was in geology. That's how I became a geologist! But after all these years I really have no regrets. I think I would have been really good in whatever I had chosen because I am a workaholic. I don't do things fifty per cent. I do them one hundred per cent or I don't do them at all. I am such a person.

I would have been really good in whatever I had chosen because I am a workaholic. I don't do things fifty per cent. I do them one hundred per cent or I don't do them at all.

At the University of Belgrade, Faculty of Geology and Mineralogy, the men didn't like women in the field at first. Somehow they had the impression that women are delicate, fine creatures who cannot stand physical effort and climbing and having all these rucksacks full of rocks on their shoulders. So even though the government had given us equality, we still had to fight for it sometimes. You had to make sure that you got what you had the right to get. Before the war geology was mainly a male field, but after the war everybody did what they could do. There were forty-nine per cent women in geology when I started.

As a woman geologist . . . you absolutely have to share the work equally . . . If you are consistent within these rules you really get respect.

Deep in his heart our professor really disapproved of girls in the field. He always called us trouble-makers. After first year we had to go to the fields. Our group consisted of nine geologists, seven men and two women. I was one of them. He absolutely hated every minute of seeing us there. He took us to one of the coal-mines in eastern Serbia. Two mines were connected undergroud by a narrow passage. The distance between them was nine kilometres underground. He didn't use the lift to take us down. We had to use the ladders. I had a hard hat, a lamp, a hammer, and men's rubber boots. I was very slim, about forty-six kilograms [seven stones two pounds] and these boots went up to my knees. I had to go down the ladder and I didn't know I needed at least two hands more to cope with the lamp, the hammer, this slippery ladder and the dark. You couldn't stop because the next second somebody would be on your hands. So you had to go in rhythm. The miners really hate women underground. They think it is bad luck. So we hid our hair under these hard hats. The miners said about me, 'Why did you take this poor little boy with you?' Anyway, this poor little boy had to go underground for nine kilometres to reach the other mine and then climb up all these ladders again. The worst thing was that there was too much water underground and some of the holes that we had to go through were so low that we had to lie on our backs and slowly move our bodies through them. Mice were running over our faces. It was an absolutely incredible experience.

It was pitch dark when we came out. My girlfriend and I had a room to ourselves. We had no strength to get rid of our overalls and boots. We just dropped dead in our beds, and put our pillows under our legs. Everything was shaking like a jelly. After a couple of hours our professor came to see us because he felt really guilty. The boys had almost collapsed. He said, 'Why did you put your pillows under your legs instead of under your head?' My friend said, 'Because it's not the legs' fault that they are here, the head is the one who brought me here.' He talked to students about that for generations. He always asked them, 'Where are you going to put your pillows?' He said to us, 'Now you have time to think it over. That is geology. If you can take it, that's it. Don't complain tomorrow.' Of course no one dropped geology because it is so fascinating. Once you start to understand and read the rocks it is really an open book.

I was married in 1951 when I was twenty-two and still a student. In Yugoslavia the conditions were terrible. The majority of buildings in Belgrade were destroyed during the war, so accommodation was almost impossible. We lived for four years in a small servant's room in a big apartment which belonged to somebody else. A servant's room was two metres by two metres. It was a pretty hard life. My husband had a good scholarship and money from demonstrating. On the basis of that we calculated we could live. I lost my scholarship when I married. Eventually we got an apartment, and we had a beautiful son. My husband got his PhD with the highest marks ever. He was the youngest PhD in Belgrade University. I worked a lot on that helping him. Then he had to go to the army to finish his service for twelve months. When everything was fine he came back and died within three months. I was twenty-seven and my son was two and a half. I was working in the Academy of Science. I had worked all the time because my mother lived with me and she looked after the boy. So I found myself in a really bad situation. I was in debt up to my neck because I had taken my husband to Paris to see a doctor who was our only hope. But it didn't help. I had my mother who had no pension. I had a brother who was a student, my husband's brother who was a student, and I had my son. I was the only one who worked. What did I do? I spent nine months out of twelve in the field because you got extra money for that. So we survived. My brother got a degree in law, my brother-in-law got a degree in dentistry.

I was the only one who worked. What did I do? I spent nine months out of twelve in the field because you got extra money for that. So we survived.

I was absolutely crazy. I hated everybody. I was walking in

the city seeing old crippled people and I hated them because he was only thirty years and seven days old when he died. But I just had to live and keep going. Too many people were dependent on me. I had no time for the luxury of suffering. I can tell you one thing – you survive only if you have some satisfaction from somewhere. For me it was my work.

One day after my husband's death I was working in a very deep creek. It was absolutely without light because it was so dense with vegetation. All of a sudden I was totally overcome with pain. My biggest problem had been that I couldn't cry. Suddenly it got me. I sat in this creek and I cried and cried and cried. A very old gypsy woman who was looking after sheep appeared out of nowhere and said, 'What's happened to you?' I told her everything, just everything. She looked at me and in a very heavy gypsy accent said, 'Are you crazy or something? He cannot be dead. As long as you think of him he can't be dead, he's alive. He looks through your eyes, he sees everything. When you see something, just stand for a second and think about him and he has seen it.' I thought, 'That's incredible. He's alive as long as I live.' I have never forgotten this old woman. So, that is the first part of my life.

I was too young to stay a widow. I just had to get married because being a widow at the age of twenty-seven you are very vulnerable. Everybody wants to 'help' you, you know? So I was very lucky to meet my husband who was a mining engineer. I went to visit a friend of mine, a geologist, and they worked together. I knew the first evening that I was going to marry him. It was just meant to be. So I had my little beautiful daughter with him and to see my children brother and sister, oh boy, that was something. I'm very grateful to my husband because my son and he have such a close relationship. Even now, when my son is twenty-seven and a man in his own right, they are really good friends. You have to put a lot in to get something back but sometimes you put everything in and you don't get anything back. I was just lucky.

In Yugoslavia everything is so well organised. You have two months off before you have your baby, and then another two months to stay full time with the baby. Then for a year you have only four hours' daily work, so you can feed it. Yes, four hours a day with full salary, superannuation and everything else. All medical care is free anyway. That's for everybody who works. After eleven months or a year you get a certificate from your doctor saying the baby needs its mother a little bit longer. So you have another ten or twelve months at home, and the children really don't suffer in this first stage. There are a lot of good things in Yugoslavia. It's just that we weren't happy in those first days. It was really a country without law.

My mother's dream was a warm home and waiting for my father . . . I tried to follow her main idea. But I also wanted a career. I didn't see why I couldn't have both. So I did.

Well, we lived in Belgrade, where I was involved in pure research, until 1968. Then opportunities came across our path and we decided to go to Africa because we had a very good offer from an Anglo-American corporation. Then we came to Australia. The only place in my experience in Australia where I am not treated as a second class citizen is where I work. It's a good department with very international attitudes. I don't do any teaching at all, I am museum curator. I am the person in charge of all the collections, which are the biggest within Australian universities. We have about 180 000 specimens and about 100 000 of them are for teaching. It is really the best collection I have ever seen at any university, and I have seen a lot.

The school is very strong so our students have no problems in finding jobs. The number of girl students increases every year. Before the war there were very few. They are very interested to find out from me what it was like to work in the field in Europe, where it is quite different. Here it's always an expedition – everything is so far away and every ordinary trip to the field is an excitement and quite a big deal. You have to organise everything from water to medicines. I think field-work is beautiful. Once you go there, that's it. You are hooked.

As a woman geologist you are accepted when they realise after a couple of years that you are not trying to get it easy. But you have to make the rules within yourself to get the respect. You absolutely have to share the work equally. When you are in the field never let them use you as a housewife or a servant to fix their buttons or cook the meals every day. You cook the meals when your turn comes. If you are consistent within these rules you really get respect. I volunteered always for the longest tours and never let them feel sorry for me. As my husband was in a similar profession, he understood it had to be like that.

Australia is absolutely fascinating, especially for a geologist. To put an age on the rocks like three thousand one hundred million years is really exciting. In the Flinders Ranges we have found one of the oldest and most beautiful fossil fauna. It's six hundred million years old. I specialised in the field of old rocks before I became a consultant.

Last Sunday, I had a group of doctors from the Royal Adelaide Hospital and a visiting professor from America. His hobby is geology. I took them to the museum. Then we had a barbecue in McLaren Vale and after that I took them to Hallet Cove to the field. They just couldn't believe how simple it all is once you have the explanation. I loved every minute of it. As with all other subjects, the more you know the more you realise how little you know. There is always another door to be opened. I will stay here until I retire. I think I will be remembered for doing a decent job. I have never left work without thinking, 'Have I really done everything I should?'

My husband and I are both very professional people. We respect each other's career and help each other. If I am sick and stay two days at home I get mad. I have to go back to work. I don't know what to do with myself at home. My mother was one of these beautiful modest girls made for home. She had an education but she never worked. Her dream was a warm home and waiting for my father every day at the gate. It was beautiful to see them. I tried to follow her main idea. But I also wanted a career. I didn't see why I couldn't have both. So I did. I'm not the only one. My sister went through the same thing. My brother's wife is a professional woman, and they have two children. They don't even have the help of my mother which I was lucky to have. They just put the children in a crêche, and everybody is happy.

They do all the housework, then they work during the day and the husband does nothing. It's the women's mistake if they do it all. They should never accept such conditions.

Although I do all the jobs at home with the family, sharing the work, I still can't see myself as a housewife. I've never had to do two jobs like many women do. They do all the housework, then they work during the day and the husband does nothing. It's the women's mistake if they do it all. They should never accept such conditions. I would never let that happen to me. Why should I? I can earn my piece of bread. If I don't get understanding in my marriage where can I expect to get it? At home we are absolutely well organised. We share everything. There is one rule in the family and that is we never push anyone to do the jobs they hate. That's how you win. For instance, my husband would never dry the dishes. He will wash always but don't ask him to dry. I cannot see the needle – that's my daughter's job. With the children studying and two of us working full time, you just cannot let one person do the whole lot. That was never a problem with us.

If you have in mind that the only thing which is important is the progress of science . . . you have done your job.

Since I've lived here I've seen more and more women who prefer to work after they are married. Women want careers as well but they often have to fight husbands who want housewives. Often the women and children come third with the husband – after the car and the pub. If women don't like it, they will have to fight it. Women in Australia have a long way to go. They have to make that a long term permanent project. There's no way that they can achieve something in one year and then forget and sleep on it. The girls who are studying now and getting degrees know exactly what they want. They are getting married but they delay having children because they wish to achieve some experience in their fields before enjoying motherhood for a while. But if they don't follow their fields for four or five years, they are out. Technology changes everything so quickly now. That is where the women who have responsible jobs should really help them, through seminars or short courses, so that they can catch up and come back to the market. I didn't need to do this because I have been working twenty-six years full time.

My advice to younger women in the sciences is firstly to work hard, and not to expect very quick success. Research is ten per cent novelty and ninety per cent routine. Everybody who starts in research thinks every day they will discover a new law. It is not so. You have to go through a million routine jobs that are boring and depressing in order to achieve something. You will maybe spend years and years without achieving anything new but one day it will come. If not in your time, the work you have done will be a base for somebody else to achieve the results. So if you don't take it very personally, if you have in mind that the only thing which is important is the progess of science, if you see yourself just as one small cog in the whole process, and if you are not so ambitious to achieve everything for yourself, you have done your job.

In 1974, when I first came to Australia I was amazed at how women were treated, especially migrant women. The racism is unbelievable. One day I was walking along North Terrace with my children. I had just arrived from Melbourne. I was very proud. I had been a citizen of Adelaide for a full two weeks and I wanted to show the children North Terrace, the university and all the monuments. Suddenly we were stopped by three Adelaide citizens and we were told, 'Piss off wogs, bloody migrants, making North Terrace dirty and filthy.' They abused us like this for no reason whatsoever, except that we were talking another language. I freely became an Australian citizen. My son now has an Australian wife and my daughter has an Australian boyfriend. What am I going to do in the old country? My country is where my children are.

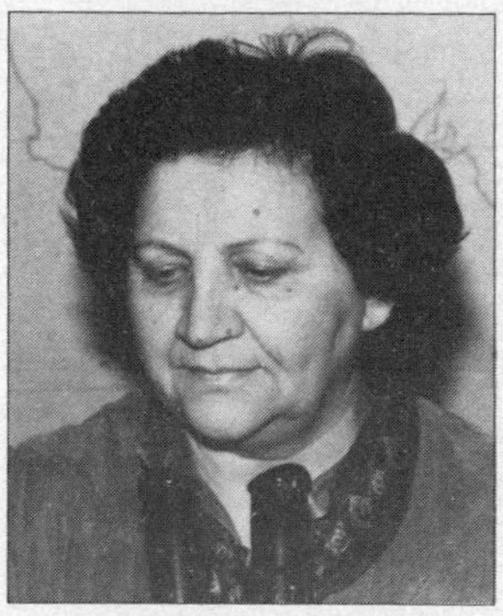

What hope do I see for migrant women in this country? To be honest, nothing for the first generation. They have to finish in the factories or in their little backyards. I have seen a few of the women of my age who work in factories – they will never know English. What's happening to the migrants without language, who are illiterate in their own countries, coming here? They are condemned to life in ghettos. The women are going crazy. Until recently migrant interpreter services and all migrant affairs really belonged to Australians who didn't speak anything but English. It's incredible. The government provides the service, but there is no contact with the community. So that's what we privately do for our people. We tell them the name of a good lawyer, a good real estate agent, and a good doctor who has patience and understanding and compassion. Because we are emotional people a nice word means much more than pills. I have no regrets about being emotional. I think it is beautiful.

The second generation is in a much better position, because they already belong more to this country, although they still have problems. I have great hopes because the young people are different. They mix with migrants without prejudice. My son's friends explore different cuisines, they cook themselves, they invite people for dinner parties. You couldn't find that fifteen years ago. From your history and a few of your writers I get the impression that very few people could afford to travel before the war. Being so isolated and being under the British for so long, you really didn't build up your confidence. But today young people travel a lot and see Renaissance Italy and monuments and Michaelangelo, so they think twice before they call Italians names when they come back. Subconsciously they build up a respect for something they didn't quite realise. Because economic conditions guide people to leave their own country, it doesn't mean that they are bad people.

But don't forget one terrible thing. In such families, the children are ashamed of their parents. I have seen that many times. It breaks my heart. The parents who were washing the floors, and doing the dirtiest jobs to give their children opportunities, withdraw themselves before they are told to go, because the children are ashamed of the parents with the terrible broken English, with different manners, with different ideas. It's not easy for anybody. The children suffer because they feel guilty. They know that their parents deserve a better share of their success but at the same time they have been laughed at too often.

A feminist? I never understood the word really. If you have in mind fighting for women's rights in a quiet, persistent way, yes I am.

I don't think that Australian men are really good husbands. They don't encourage their wives to fulfill their potential. Their own needs always come first, then the children and finally the wife. Change is a long process. A feminist? I never understood the word really. If you have in mind fighting for women's rights in a quiet, persistent way, yes I am. I think the worst damage to women's movements is done by the extremists. Perhaps in a sleepy community like Australia – I call it that because everybody's dead scared of changes – maybe in such circumstances you need some extremists, but in the long run the quiet, persistent stand of women, especially women who have a say and have positions of power, will produce the results. My daughter a feminist? Oh, she went through so many different stages in growing up. She was very religious at one stage. She's atheist at the moment. God knows what she's going to do next. She is a very open child who, just like her mother, says everything she has on her mind regardless of the consequences. She's very often in trouble for that, but we encouraged her to have her opinions.

All my life I have been a sort of a rebel, but in a positive way – like being first in the river after the winter; like supporting somebody who is on the black list and taking him for a walk in front of everybody; like going to the church when you are not a believer but you want to show that you are not scared of going – this is the sort of rebel I was. I react spontaneously to injustice. I can't take it. I have no respect for myself if I witness something which is really nasty and I haven't tried to help the people or the person to whom the injustice is done. I really feel terrible. The greatest injustice in Australia is the treatment of Aborigines. It's just incredible. By giving them money the feeling of guilt disappears. The money doesn't solve their problems, it creates problems. That is a very dark side of Australia in my opinion. Literally.

If I had to describe an Australian in one word, it would be 'shy'. Shy to show feelings, shy to fight when one should, shy to cry, shy to jump with joy, shy to show off if you have the reasons for it. It's not natural. I know we are a very loud lot for Australians – they call my family the kissing Stojanovics because we kiss each other ten times, sometimes twenty or fifty times a day. We kiss our friends, men and women equally. My Australian daughter-in-law took a while to get used to us. Now she gets most upset if I don't give her as many kisses as all the others. Australian women are more repressed than men. I suppose it's a reflection of how they are treated. They're a long way down on the list. So they have even less confidence. As I said before, they have to fight quietly but they have to do it all the time, not episodically. They have to keep up the struggle. And they should kiss and hug each other more. Perhaps that's one of the things that they can learn from Europeans.

Now I wish to spend more time with my family because the children are leaving. I have done enough in my career to be satisfied and happy with it. My son has an honours degree in biochemistry from the University of Adelaide. He has a job with the Waite Institute. My daughter is the only person in the family in the Arts. She is studying drama and philosophy. She is our thinker. We always encouraged our children to do what they wanted. She was too young when she matriculated, she wasn't seventeen. With our background we don't like early decisions, so we sent her to Europe for a year. She travelled all by herself making her base in Belgrade. She had the time of her life.

My husband is the best friend I ever had. I refuse to go without him and travel like we did before. We used to have separate holidays to be free to do everything you want when you want, and how you want. You always have an obligation if you are together. You get tired of each other. We found it was very good to have a break. So I went twice to Europe without him. You don't do that if you are insecure. You can do it only if you are safe. We have never been jealous of anything. It's an unknown feeling to us, because we don't lie to each other. Honesty is the most important thing. It is the only healthy base for everything you build up. Our number one priority in spending money is travelling. We never have any money. We have the same taste. In a huge shop with a million things on display we will go to the same thing together at the same moment. It didn't come with the years spent together. We have always been inclined to like the same artists, the same type of films, the same type of book. Travelling is our biggest joy, and the children are just the same. Our anniversary is on Monday and I'm giving my husband a clarinet. He never had the opportunity to learn to play clarinet. He's the same age as me, fifty-three. He is chasing his dreams, and why not? I would like to spend two or three years travelling – just travelling and stopping where we feel like stopping. We never could afford that. When we retire we are going to do it.

Over a cup of tea in her tiny office next to the museum Mima apologised for weeping when she had recalled certain past events in her life. I thanked her for being prepared to re-live such painful experiences. She said, 'I didn't want to embarrass you. So many of my Australian friends look uncomfortable when I show my emotions so freely. If you feel it, why not show it? What is there to be ashamed of? I can't hide my feelings and I must always be true to myself, yes?'

Her husband arrived to pick her up after work. He told me how proud he was of her and why he thinks it is important that her story is told.

When I finally said goodbye I kissed her. With Mima, it seemed only natural.

ROBYN NEVIN (Actress)
Robyn had clearly prepared herself for the interview. She was wearing a crisply ironed silk blouse and skirt. A bunch of carefully arranged flowers faced me on the table. The stage was set. I turned on the tape-recorder. Nothing. I blushed and stammered and flicked switches as if my life depended on it. The greatest fear of any interviewer was hovering above me. After twenty minutes of semi-hysterical attempts to get the machine to work I gave up and pleaded for another time. Robyn covered up what must have been annoyance and said she could squeeze in a lunch-time interview between rehearsals at the Opera House.

Having had the tape-recorder fixed I checked it at least ten times before she arrived. We had a few drinks and sandwiches in my hotel room. Robyn was relaxed and to some extent off-guard – perhaps the breakdown of the recorder had been a bonus.

There's a part of me that always operates as an observer. I stare at people in buses all the time. Companions in restaurants often say, 'Are you listening to me or are you more interested in the people at the next table?' I say, 'I'm more interested in the people at the next table.' I listen and watch and absorb. I'm more of an observer than a doer. I'm not saying that's good or bad, though it can make life very difficult, but I'm extremely sensitive to mood, atmosphere and other people's emotional conditions. Generally women are more sensitive than men, but I think I am even more so. I'm very big on sub-text.

All the world really is a stage. Children start off so open, honest and clear in their responses but gradually learn to be the same as adults – devious, manipulative and deceitful – in order to survive. You learn to add layers and layers and layers on top of your personality so that you end up with some kind of image. The difficulty for actors is shedding all those layers so they can take on the layers of the character that they're playing in a very calculated skilled way.

It's crazy isn't it? No one would ever say that a male actor was brave because he allowed himself to look plain.

One of my pet subjects is the distinction between actors and what I call personality performers. Personality performers are those who have a certain type of personality that they impose on whatever character they're playing, so that if that personality becomes popular, audiences actually go to see only that personality. On the other hand true actors are often not recognisable from play to play because they dispense with their own physical mannerisms and speech patterns. They try to rid themselves of their own social persona, so that they are in fact acting. A really crass example is an actress who, no matter what part she's playing, will still wear the kind of make-up of the day that suits her. You see her wearing it in press photographs or in the foyer on first nights. She'll have the same kind of hair-style so that the audience is still comfortable with its image of her as that attractive vibrant personality they know from the *Don Lane Show* or whatever. Whereas an actress playing any one of a number of roles will create a character that will have a special look, that may in fact require a very plain appearance. Somebody said to me the other day, 'I think it's very brave when actresses allow themselves to look really plain on television.' I know exactly what they meant. The public is used to that constant, comfortable, plastic finish that's promoted, particularly for women. It's crazy, isn't it? No one would ever say that a male actor was brave because he allowed himself to look plain.

A man reaches the age of thirty-eight, forty-five or fifty-five and he's at the peak of his virility. He's mature and interesting and his craggy lined face is more and more attractive to women. But the female equivalent is not considered desirable on any level really. You have to accept it if that's the attitude of the country you choose to live in, and although you love your country for many good reasons, there are always a couple of nasty attitudes like that. I'm sure if I'd been brought up in America I would have had a face-lift by now because that's the tradition there. Or I would have spent the last twenty years working on my face and my body so that it didn't deteriorate to the extent that it clearly has. And in European countries ageing wouldn't be a problem at all. I'd be accepted as I was, and used for important things like talent. The trend will change because we follow American trends, and stories about mature women will be made here. Probably by then I'll be in the next age group!

I've never really had ambitions to play any particular roles though I've recently become very interested in comedy, having always been cast as strong tragic women. I think that has something to do with a residue of pain left from my childhood.

I remember myself as a very quiet private child, not outgoing at all, with a very rich fantasy world, gleaned from books which I adored. When I was very small I used to read with a torch under the bedclothes. I learned books off by heart and recited them. Acting was something that evolved from my school experiences. It was a school in Hobart called Farne. I went back there recently to talk to the girls. It's exactly the same – still only 300 pupils – a very gentle, conservative school. When I was there it was run by two elderly, refined ladies. One of them was also the English mistress, and her main interest during the year was to produce the school play. She would adapt famous fairy stories or classic tales into plays. One year she did *Snow White and the Seven Dwarfs*. Because I was a very good reader, and small and pretty with very dark hair and pale skin, she cast me as Snow White. That's really how it began. From then on she gave me the lead in school plays so I didn't have to do compulsory sports, which were always a problem to me. Acting was where I shone at school. It was my form of self-expression.

One morning a prospectus for the National Institute of Dramatic Art (NIDA) was held up at assembly. Those girls who were interested were told to go to the headmistress' study. I carried this prospectus around with me for a couple of weeks, and then my parents talked to the headmistress. Auditions were held in Tasmania. I did Cleopatra's dying speech from Shakespeare's *Anthony and Cleopatra*, just because it was a long, dramatic speech. I was chosen. And I was emotionally ready to leave school. That was in 1959 and NIDA had just started.

My father was the managing director of the Dunlop Rubber Company in Victoria. Until I was eleven we lived in one of those big old Melbourne houses. I recently went back to have a look at it. It's still intact. It has turrets and brightly painted wooden balconies and a very big garden full of camellias, hydrangeas and English trees. My mother didn't work. She devoted her entire energies to her daughters and husband. I was a fairly late baby so my mother always seemed to me to be quite an old woman. My next sister is five years older than me and the next one is a lot older. When I was a child the gap seemed huge. My parents broke up when I was eleven. We moved to Tasmania as a sort of retreat and my mother became a single mother with three daughters.

I suppose this situation lasted only a few years and then my father returned. The problems continued. My mother's single objective in those years was to maintain an appearance of normality and calm. She hoped that an outsider looking in would see that we were a perfectly respectable, ordinary, middle class family. I'm sure a lot of families have this veneer, whereas within the family structure there is actually incredible conflict and tension. There was always a level of drama attached to our lives because of that family situation. But it was all going on under the surface. No wonder I'm so keen on sub-text!

I didn't include my peers in my home life. I isolated myself. I remember having days at school when I was extremely tearful. I'd be very emotionally distressed without ever knowing why. If ever there was a hint of, 'What's the matter?' I'd withdraw. An awful lot of my emotional conflict and confusion was never resolved as a child, and every now and then the tension that was always there would erupt. Most of the time things weren't discussed because my mother wanted to maintain this pretence. It's terribly interesting when you think about why somebody becomes an actress.

I'm a person who is always torn between reasoning things out and trusting instincts. I would prefer to operate through the intellect alone. There's this constant battle going on. That's why I don't like that theory that people become actors so they can work out their emotional problems on stage in front of an audience. I loathe that self-indulgent acting where the actor cries instead of the audience. It's the actor's job to make the audience cry, if that's what the author wants. It's not the actor's job to sit up there and have a good bawl and work a few things out. I think that's really boring.

The actor's first responsibility is to understand the play or the text, then, during rehearsals, to explore the emotional situation of the character within the context of the play. I've wept in some rehearsals but having done that, can recreate it without going through the emotion again every night for eight weeks. You develop skills that hopefully will provoke the emotion in the audience. Once you reach performance level most of your concentration should be almost outside of yourself looking in. But I'm like that all the time. I remember an emotional period in my domestic life when I experienced extreme fear, and I thought at the time, 'So that's what my body does.' I've recreated that exact physical response on stage because I know that's what happens in real life.

I'm awfully bored with that aura of pain and tragedy that I seem to project. At one stage I lived with a very famous Sydney identity who ran a boarding house. I was just out of NIDA and must have been feeling particularly sorry for myself. I was telling her this tragic story, and she thought it was the funniest thing she'd ever heard. She laughed so much she literally wet her pants! I got a terrific fright. It was really good for me.

You have to develop an awareness, an objectivity, and work on that rather than staying stuck in the pain of the past.

That was the beginning of my learning that you can't go on hanging on to your tragic past. I recently recorded a *Poets' Tongue* programme for the ABC and was reading poems by a New Zealander. The narrator was relating the poet's life story and he said something like, 'On 4 August she married and a week later she left him to live with another man whose baby she was actually having. Two weeks later she had a miscarriage, then she went to join a nunnery where she had a nervous breakdown.' It went on and on with this stream of tragic events. I got the giggles and thought, 'Gosh, that's just like that time Chica laughed at my tragedy.' You have to develop an awareness, an objectivity, and work on that rather than staying stuck in the pain of the past.

It was very exciting being one of the first batch of really trained actors to come out of Australia. We'd done two presentation production plays at the end of the year. Everyone from the profession came to see them and some of us might be offered jobs. On the last day at NIDA, Professor Robert Quentin took a crumpled old envelope out of his pocket and said, 'Now, here are the jobs that some of you students have been offered.'

I was tentatively offered a six months' contract with the ABC as a sort of apprentice to one of those up-front ABC women. I was furious. My sole ambition in life was to be contracted to the Young Elizabethan Players. I was very young and idealistic. I refused the ABC offer.

The following Monday morning I got a call from the Trust Players, which was the big company in Sydney then. I walked up to Kings Cross to borrow a shilling from one of the other students for my fare into town. I went in and they said, 'We'd like to offer you a contract with the Trust Players as an understudy, playing small parts, etc. This is the accountant, this is Miss Robyn Nevin, sign the contract, here's a cheque straight away for a retainer. You'll start in a couple of weeks.' It was one of those extraordinary instant success stories. Ironically I became a television presentation announcer some years later when I gave up the theatre.

I worked with the Players for ten pounds a week as an understudy for about a year, then I went to the second Adelaide Festival of Arts, when acclaimed Australian actress Zoe Caldwell was doing St Joan. I was a page-boy. After touring with that company for some time I was asked if I'd fly up to Rockhampton to replace an actress who'd been on tour with the Young Elizabethan Players, my ideal company. I leaped at it. Little did I know that I'd be playing on table tops and travelling through the outback under the most extraordinary conditions, being pelted with Jaffas and Minties by kids who hated the standard of what we were doing. It was very badly edited Shakespeare, and we were a lot of grumpy, discontented people who'd been touring on a little bus. We used to arrive in a town and set up the scenery ourselves, do the whole thing ourselves, then pack it all up, get in the bus, drive to another town and do it again. It was terribly difficult and didn't seem to have anything to do with what I thought it was all about. So I gave it up.

Through a series of circumstances I became involved in the crass commercial world of photography and advertising. I worked for a famous fashion photographer. It's amazing that this should have happened to me because it was so unsuitable. But true to form, I applied myself with dedication and worked terribly hard. He thought I was terrific and I stayed there for about a year, until I became totally disillusioned. So I went home to Tasmania and got the job with the ABC as a presentation announcer. That really led me into getting married and because I met my husband there, I stayed on at the ABC and won a couple of Logie awards.

Then we lived in London for two years and I had my child. I worked for a repertory company run by a shark and a charlatan, who was married to a very famous musical comedy star. He treated her appallingly. We had a terrible fight in Torquay because he was screwing all the girls in the cast. He just took one look at my thin lips and knew he wouldn't get anywhere near me. So there was an immediate conflict. He worked very hard to put me down in front of the company. I ended up leaving on the midnight express, back to London. I rang up Equity Actors' Union the next morning and they said, 'Oh, not another complaint about so and so.' When we came back to Australia we separated. My baby was about four months old. That's when I started again in the theatre. I had to make a living for the two of us. Now I look upon that time as if I was semi-conscious. It's extraordinary to look back at a man you married in 1965 and think, 'But who was the person who married him?' I can't relate to that person at all, which is why I always get awfully concerned about people who marry so young.

When we came back to Australia we separated. My baby was about four months old. That's when I started again in the theatre. I had to make a living for the two of us.

I was twenty-two when I married and I've had eleven years of struggle. In those days it was particularly difficult and I had some bad experiences. I came to Sydney to do a post-graduate course at NIDA and left my daughter with my family while I established myself. I remember being interviewed by a woman in one of the baby care centres I was checking out. A baby was lying in a sort of cradle in her office. When the

woman, who I didn't warm to at all, left the room I went over and looked at the baby. It was lying in a pooey nappy, had a rash and looked hideous. I started to weep. She came back in and said, 'Look dear, just go away and get yourself together. Then come back and we'll talk about it sensibly.'

I got married again in 1975. All in all, the relationship lasted about three years. It was a very impulsive marriage. I responded totally to a person who seemed to have extraordinary qualities. I'm always attracted to people with qualities like energy, a sense of life, a good intellect, and humour. It was playwright Jim McNeil. I met him four days after he'd got out of prison, because I was in *How Does Your Garden Grow?*, the play that was presented to coincide with his release from jail. Director John Bell had asked, 'Will you do this for us Robyn? It's awfully small but it's a terrific play.' I'd seen two of his plays before and thought they were wonderful. It was a hideously difficult part to play. It wasn't well written, particularly the woman's role. So Jim and I met and became very close, very quickly. It was just one of those things where you go bang. But it obviously happened at a time of my life when I needed some kind of bonding situation, or I felt ready for it.

There are other times when I just withdraw from any possibility of emotional involvement, which is quite healthy for me. I have good periods when I'm totally on my own, independent of any one-to-one relationship, when I just establish myself again and consolidate my centre which gets a bit scattered in this business. The pressures of being a mother and an actress are great and do sometimes leave me really tired and feeling as if I haven't been given anything. Giving to 500 people and the cast on stage for a concentrated period of the day can be very draining.

Everybody in the theatre treats everybody the same. It's talent that counts.

I don't think the performing arts in this country are considered as necessary to us as human beings as I believe they are. In other parts of the world they are vital to the life of a community. I've done countless plays at a little theatre called Jane Street, which is out at Randwick. I've done plays at the Nimrod when it first started in Kings Cross, and I've done things that an awful lot of people have never heard of. I've acted in hundreds of plays – about as many as houses that I've lived in. They've all taken an awful lot out of me. In an historical sense I've contributed a great deal over the past eleven years to the theatre community in this city. I'm certainly receiving respect and accolades and those sorts of things now. Unfortunately, in the meantime I got a bit cynical and angry that what I and my peers are all trying to do is not necessarily wanted. Perhaps that's just the curse of the artist, the problem of being a creative person in this society.

Do actresses get a particularly tough deal in Australia? Well, in the theatre there are wonderful roles for women. The subsidised theatre companies do literature right through the ages. Terrific roles have been and are being written for women. The commercial area is the problem. It's the same in the film industry. It's difficult for women of my age. It's even difficult for somebody like Wendy Hughes who is extremely beautiful and young and a good actress. If she was in Hollywood and had the status there that she has here, she'd be doing one wonderful film after another. Here good roles don't exist for women around that thirty-ish age group. Most of the roles she plays are, I think, token sex symbols. It's much easier for people like Judy Davis who are that bit younger. Those years make all the difference in Australia.

Historically men have always controlled the direction of the theatre. However, changes in women's roles are occurring . . . and it is spreading to the theatre.

One of the other problems in the theatre as far as women are concerned is the fact that most directors are homosexual. I realise it's a very delicate topic. I'm not referring to someone's sexual preference but the way in which that sexual preference influences the material, particularly in terms of women's roles. For example, there was a play that, shall I say, I knew very well. I saw it directed by a very strong, sensible woman. Then I saw the same play directed by a very intelligent friend of mine, who is homosexual. Under his direction it became sickening schmaltz. He took all the toughness out of it and turned it into a really self-indulgent, sentimental evening. The difference between those two productions helped confirm the instinctive feelings that were evolving in me about the ways in which homosexual directors actually soften women's roles. Perhaps a different kind of distortion happens with heterosexual male directors, but I've worked with so few of them I couldn't speak with the same kind of knowledge.

I'm actually about to direct a play myself and I know of three other women who are heading the same way. Richard Wherrett, Director of the Sydney Theatre Company, is making a space for women to become assistant directors. It's wonderful. Another problem with directors is that many of them are academics who have never been actors. Historically of course, men have always controlled the direction of the theatre. However, changes in women's roles are occurring right across the board and it is spreading to the theatre. Women are already making good changes in terms of more plays about women or by women and there's all kinds of theatre available now. In an overall sense, theatre does reflect what's happening in the community. It's often a question of taste and the public will ultimately determine how long they will last.

As for the casting couch routine – I always hated flirting. I couldn't understand the kind of role that you were supposed to play as a female. So I didn't. I've always been aware that those manipulative games are silly. Your first responsibility is to the play and whatever the play is trying to say. I'm fairly preoccupied with balance in all things. I always like to show, even if it's only sub-textually, reasons why a person may be the way they are. But I never judge the character. If you think, 'Oh, I loathe that character,' you often tend to play the judgement rather than the character.

I believe that all the arts have a responsibility to nurture the finest sensibilities in people. But the people who own and run the television channels aren't in the business to feed the souls and spirits of the public. They mainly aim at teenagers who will buy their products to keep their television channels going. That's a very unhappy and cynical situation. It's largely why I don't like working in television and I don't like my child watching it. All I'm asking for is a balanced situation where the public have a choice – not between one quiz show and another or one soapy and another, but between a soapy and a programme on the life of somebody who contributed wonderfully to the world, or a play that we can learn something about ourselves from. The kind of theatre and movies that I love are those that really do increase my awareness and understanding of me and everybody else. This means comedy as well as tragedy. We especially need these now because we are so busy earning livings and rushing around under all sorts of frightening pressures. Life is getting tougher and tougher. We need time to pause, to listen to, look at and absorb soul food, and to look at the way we're living and the quality of our lives.

There's a terrible actress in Sydney who is ambitious to be a personality and a star and to lead that kind of life. Somebody said to me, 'That person is in every single magazine and newspaper I pick up but I've never seen her on stage.' I said, 'Well, that's what she spends all her energy doing, promoting herself as a personality.' It is possible to do that. It depends on your priorities and what you want to contribute. You can choose to exist on the circuit that provides personalities with work, the large circuit that makes money, and gives prestige, and fame and all those silly things. It's not for me.

I want to be very good at what I do and I want to be known for that. Fame has all sorts of unattractive connotations to me. I was once walking with a television actor down a street in Charters Towers in Queensland. Even in the outback of Queensland, people would not let that man alone. I'd worked for as many years and done as much work, but not on television. I was able to walk down the street and I didn't have to wear sunglasses, or hide in pubs. He was practically torn apart. I would loathe that kind of attitude shown towards me. When *Water Under the Bridge* was screened on television it certainly brought recognition, but a different kind of recognition from just being seen on television a lot. I wasn't a personality and the programme was a ratings disaster. But it was a critical success and people admired what I was doing as an actress. I responded to that very happily.

The sorts of failures that I've had have been only in a commercial sense really. I was in a play at the Sydney Opera House a few years ago that was a very, very bad production. I knew from the first day it was going to be appallingly bad. What angered me was that the person who was in control of that situation, the director, was ever allowed to be there. It was very hard for me to get up night after night and perform on that stage knowing that people had paid ten dollars a seat to see something that I could have told them not to come to. I didn't take it as a personal failure, I took it as a failure of the entire situation. Once I was in a play with an actor who could not allow anybody else on stage to have any time of their own. He constantly worked very hard to distract the audience whenever he was on stage. I thought that was so silly because if you allow that other person to be good, when your turn comes and you contribute as you are supposed to do, then the whole thing will be good and you'll come off awfully well. What's the point in fussing around the stage making a complete idiot of yourself when you're not only ruining the situation for the audience and the rest of the cast, but ultimately for yourself as well? The cleverest thing you can do on stage is to be absolutely still. Then most people will watch you most of the time. You are there to present a play to an audience, not to present yourself to an audience.

The future? I know I'll always be an actress but I look forward to doing some directing as well. Marriage? You just have to take it as it comes. I actually like being married in that I like sharing. If I was to marry again, he'd have to be quite a remarkable man. It's difficult to be married to an actress. But then the demands that men in high power positions have upon them are also enormous. It's very good to be in a situation with somebody who is equally as preoccupied as you are. I've had problems with men who've actually been jealous of my work, and the energy that I give to it. I couldn't be bothered with anybody like that again.

I'm usually the one who's out of the dressing room first and home to relieve the babysitter. My child has been a stabilising factor in my life.

I don't mix socially with actors very much. I can't be bothered with those actors who have not only built up all those layers I was talking about before, but who've added theatrical layers. I find those clichés all a bit off-putting. I have a lot of friends who work outside the theatre with whom I spend time. I like concerts and I love reading. I spend a lot of time with my child too. I'm sure everyone imagines this wonderful theatrical whirlwind round of dinner parties and cocktail parties and first nights. It's the romance that's attached to the theatre. It's not like that at all. Most actors lead very unglamorous lives. They are really quite poor and just work all the time. But they are very late night people. Because I've had a child for twelve-

and-a-half years I haven't been able to be a late night person. I'm usually the one who is out of the dressing-room first and home to relieve the baby sitter. My child has been a stabilising factor in my life, and most actors don't have that. They go on to clubs and bars and restaurants and unwind that way. I'm quite fond of late night movies on television. If I'm in a relationship then that's a kind of companionable, relaxed time after work. I play tennis and I like picnics. I love the sun and gardening. I don't like cooking much. I don't think I'm really a typical theatrical. I'm definitely not.

Although I had attempted, as the interviewer, to pry and probe beneath the surface, the directness of Robyn's gaze often made me wonder who was observing who. It was hard to imagine that she hadn't always been so confident, so in control. I knew that she would always be an actress and never a 'personality', and wondered how long it would be before Australians recognise that actresses don't have to be younger than forty to succeed. If anyone can prove it, Robyn will.

JOY BALUCH (Mayor and businesswoman)

Joy Baluch is so far from the image you might have of the Mayor of a country town, that it's hard to know where to begin.

She said she would be in Adelaide for business and I could meet her in her small unit that she keeps in the city. It was hard for me to believe that the woman in the pink jumpsuit, with the flashing black eyes and gold gypsy earrings was really a grandmother and a Mayor. Joy is different. I guarantee that you will never meet anyone quite like her. I asked her what part she thought luck had played in her long dusty trek from the wrong side of the tracks to Mayor of the same town. Her reply will give you some idea of what to expect.

'Luck! Listen, darling. If it was raining bloody fur coats, I'd be hit by the only flying shithouse in Australia. That's how lucky I am.'

As Joy tells it, life in Port Augusta makes *Peyton Place* look like *Playschool*.

My first memory is my third birthday. I had a little cake baked by my grandmother. I was the first grandchild and was doted on, particularly by my grandfather, who was a great influence on my life. He was very majestic. Even today people say, 'How the hell did that magnificent man produce two bloody bastards like your father and your uncle?' I was his favourite. He called me Shirley Temple because of my rotten stinken curls which I tried to obscure until I was about forty-seven. I remember very vividly my little sister being brought onto the verandah in a bassinet and how I squeezed her fingers back, making her cry. When I remind her about this she says, 'You bastard. I remem-

ber that.' But I know she doesn't. I actually became a very protective sister.

From a very early age I knew I was different to boys. When I was four, I was assaulted in a big berry bush, half-way between my maternal great-grandmother's place and the beach. They tried to cover it all up but I knew that something was wrong about the berry bush. The boy would have been fourteen. Because it was never talked about, it was a mental fear. I became sexually very defensive.

My mother came from the west side of Port Augusta and my father from the east side. In those days those from the west side didn't marry those from the east. Different clans. When my father was courting my mother, there was no bridge across the Gulf. They had to catch the wool and produce ferry. If my father was late getting back he'd have to swim across the Gulf. My father is seventy-three now and he still swims every morning. I swim with him and people say, 'Oh, there's bloody mad George and his tribe.' It doesn't matter where I go. Even in parliamentary circles people say, 'Is that bloody mad father of yours still swimming every morning?' Those clans in Port Augusta still exist today. They are very bloody parochial at the grassroots level.

My maternal grandparents lived on the west side of the Great Western Bridge, and we lived on the east side with my father's parents and a little black and white spotty dog. The bridge was only wide enough for one vehicle and there were three cars in the community at that stage: one belonged to the Roman Catholic priest, naturally; one to the Anglican; and I'm buggered if I know who owned the other one. We were going across the bridge to see grandmother Parker and suddenly there were all three bloody cars. My dog ran out in front of them. My mother still declares that that's the first time I ever uttered a swear word. I got out and said, 'You rotten stinken bugger.' They can't even remember where I would have picked up such foul language. Yet today when I drop the proverbial four-letter word in front of my ninety-four-year-old grandmother she doesn't even blush.

Later, we moved to our own house in Cook. My father was a fireman with the Commonwealth Railways. I remember my mother crying with happiness in purchasing her own furniture through the Commonwealth Stores. The school at Cook hasn't changed much since then. I loved school. I came top in grade one and won the book, *Seven Little Australians*. That's one of my prized possessions. As I progressed through school everybody was bigger than me. I hated the way I looked because I was little and skinny and ugly, and I suffered endless traumas because of these corkscrew curls. I studied very hard, and I was always up in the middle. It was not until I reached high school that I got to the top, and then it was only because the numbers had dropped off.

More than anything I wanted to become a nurse, but my grandmother said that I didn't have the temperament. I was very good at shorthand, typing, book-keeping. So I left school at the age of fifteen after getting my Leaving Certificate and I commenced work in a solicitor's office for twenty-five shillings a week. The solicitor constantly roared at me. He spent all day in the pub and when old pensioners or people looking for trust account cheques came in, I would say, 'He said there's not enough in the account to write a cheque, but if you want to see him he's down there at the Flinders or the Exchange Hotel.' I sent so many of his clients there that he said to me, 'Don't bloody-well send them to the pub.' I said, 'What am I to do with them?' He'd say, 'Tell them to come back tomorrow.' I used to think, 'You bloody bastard. I'm not going to send them away. That poor lady has walked a mile and a quarter. Why shouldn't you see her now? You're only boozing down there.' Injustice always stuck in my craw. I stayed there for about four months.

I used to think, 'You bloody bastard. I'm not going to send them away. That poor lady has walked a mile and a quarter ...' Injustice always stuck in my craw.

To get into Commonwealth Railways one had to be related to St Peter, particularly if he was the Catholic St Peter, but I sent in an application and was accepted, despite the fact that my father was only an engine driver. They probably looked at my application, saw my typing and shorthand ability and that I was only sixteen and thought I could be moulded. I went into the typing pool in the chief mechanical engineering branch. It was a new office and I felt very threatened. All the women were so much older. I didn't know what shit from clay was in those days. I'm still a very good typist and at all my meetings today I take things down in shorthand. They hate that because they don't know what I'm writing. At seventeen I was appointed head typist. I don't know why, but the chief mechanical engineer said I was the only girl he'd ever known to read the general rule books during the tea-break.

I still wanted to be a nurse and at the age of seventeen and a half I sent in an application to the hospital, and I was accepted. When the letter came through, my father opened it. He opened all the mail that came in. Nothing was private. That really upset me. He said, 'If you leave your job in the Commonwealth Railways and become a nurse then don't come back into my home.' So that was the end of nursing for me. I went to see my Pop who always had a ready shoulder for me, and I said, 'I'm creating problems for my mother and father.' He said, 'There's always been problems between them.' I'd always felt this anyway.

I was never taught the facts of life. In my era it was never discussed. But I was always reminded about the berry bush. I was brought up a strict Anglican. I became a Sunday school teacher and played the organ in the church. I was terribly critical of girls who had to get married. My Nanna impressed upon me that my mother and father never had to get married. And yet somewhere at the back of my mind I knew that wasn't right. It wasn't until I was pregnant with my second child at the age of twenty-one that my sister broke the news to me at my kitchen sink. She said, 'I can do what I like, but Father won't accept anything you do. Do you know why? It was because of you he married Mother.' That was bloody hard to take. Yet I can't understand why at such an early age I had this prejudice that you had to be a virgin when you married. I think I felt, 'I've got to prove to them that I'm going to be a bloody virgin, despite the berry bush.' I didn't develop sexually until I was seventeen and then I fell in love with a boy of nineteen, but it didn't come to anything.

When I was eighteen and a half I was selected to represent Port Augusta in the Miss South Australia Quest. It was the worst day of my life. I was skinny and I still had this rotten stinken curly hair that I didn't know what to do with. I was very shy and insecure. I never told my family for a week. They were overjoyed, but no matter what they did or said it still didn't convince me. I wouldn't even tell my girlfriends. I was too ashamed. I had a very good committee. We did the fund raising and I came third in the country section. When I got to Adelaide amongst all those beauties with their swish clothes, I soon sorted out the goats from the bloody sheep. I thought, 'You might have money but some of you are bitches. I'll show you.'

It was 1950 and migration was on the scene. I started to hate the discrimination – any form of discrimination. Through the *Trans-Continental* newspaper, I read a plea for a volunteer typist to see to the needs of the migrants. So I worked at the Good Neighbour Council every Saturday morning. Because the migrants were displaced persons, they were referred to as the Balts. That's where the stigma of the Balt bastard came in. The Australian men were threatened by these men who arrived with absolutely nothing but good manners, who treated women well and were well-dressed.

In 1951 the staff clerk initiated a mechanical engineering branch ball. The head of the accounts section said, 'Who are you taking to the ball, Miss Copley?' I said, 'I'm taking Theo Baluch.' He said to me, 'When are you going to wake up to yourself and find yourself a good Australian boy?' I said, 'I haven't found one in Port Augusta who can drag himself away from the keg.' Theo was a very good dancer and I liked dancing. He wasn't attracted to me. He found me a very silly bitch. He still says I used to laugh too much. I used to dance with other migrants, unlike the other girls who had been told by their parents not to dance with those Balts. I went home with him one night, but as you didn't leave through the door with a Balt, I met him around the corner in Gladstone Square. I'm still reminded to this day that I never walked out that door with him.

I went with Theo for twelve months before my father allowed me to bring him home. I would take him to my grandmother's and Pop's place or down to the fire station where my uncle was, but I was never allowed to bring him home. If it hadn't been for the social pressures I wouldn't have married him. I had to show those bastards. There was so much animosity towards these displaced persons. Later I found out that pressures were also put on my father. People would say, 'Why do you allow a nice girl like Joy, a Sunday school teacher, to go out with him?' and they would make similar remarks to my grandparents. I hated the entrenched incestuous relationships that had produced these idiots in a population of 3 500. Yes, I married a bloody cause. I've been fighting battles all of my life – battles and lost causes.

Then the devil took a hand. I won £6 000 in a lottery. Theo had asked me to fill in the form and send it away. I called the ticket 'Two Dreamers' and I didn't think any more about it. Then at work one morning I was called out by a little messenger boy. In a country town everyone knows what's in a telegram, and he said, 'Don't fall over when you read this.' I said, 'Don't be a smart little bastard.' By that time I'd learned to swear. I opened it up and it said, 'Your ticket 14816 won £6 000 in today's consultation lottery. Congratulations.' I looked at it. I thought Natalie, my girlfriend, had played a prank on me. She was in Western Australia with the chief mechanical engineer as there had been a derailment. I went back to my desk, threw the telegram in the top drawer and got on with my typing. I went in to take shorthand. Then the assistant staff clerk came in and said to my boss, 'What are you doing working this girl to death? She's just won a lottery.' They finally convinced me that it wasn't a trick and I went out to the workshops to tell Theo. After I'd told my family I went back to work.

The previous Christmas Theo had given me a watch. I'd never had a watch and I'd always told my girlfriends that I'd marry the first man who bought me one. It was a good one. It must have taken some very hard savings. Then, when I won the lottery, I told my parents, 'Theo and I are getting married when I turn twenty-one – with or without your permission.' Winning the lottery gave me a sense of power, but I never ever outwardly displayed it. After winning I was taken down right, left and bloody centre. Anything that I wanted to buy cost double after that. Today in Port Augusta they still remember that I was the first one to ever win a lottery. What's more they think I've still got the money. They think that I'm terribly lucky, and that I got everything easy.

I gave up work in the Commonwealth Railways at the end of 1953. Theo had said that he'd wanted to leave because of the pressures that were placed upon him when we were going together. The men in the workshops gave him the shittiest jobs. They told me rotten stinken stories like he had a wife and kids back in Europe. It was terrible. They plagued him, especially after winning the lottery, and made his life hell. I became more protective of him because of these rotten bloody bastards. We had a block of land in a prime position with plans for the only two-storey house in Port Augusta. But I agreed to go to Adelaide. He didn't have a trade but he was very thrifty and had saved quite a bit of money so we bought a very big delicatessen. We employed seven people but Theo couldn't cope because of the language barrier. He'd deliver all the goods to the market gardens nearby.

Then the worst thing happened to me – I became pregnant. I was never taught about contraception. I knew literally nothing. Other than the berry bush episode, I was a virgin when I got married. Theo wouldn't have married me otherwise. At the back of my mind I always thought I shouldn't get pregnant – that nice girls didn't. Anyway, by April of 1954 I was showing signs of pregnancy which I didn't recognise. I'd always had irregular periods, so that didn't worry me, but when my boobs began discharging, I thought I was dying. I said to Theo, 'I'm going to have to go to a doctor, I'm not feeling well.' I went to our old family doctor and for years afterwards I would cover my head whenever I passed that place in case that doctor was peering out and saw me. I felt so embarrassed. When I went to see him I told him I wasn't feeling well. I said, 'I don't know why I'm not eating. I feel sick all the time.'

He said, 'Could you be pregnant?'

'No, my husband wouldn't let me get pregnant.'

'What contraceptive do you use?'

'What are contraceptives?'

'Hop on the couch.'

'What are you going to do?'

'Get undressed.'

'What for?'

'I want to examine you.'

He attacked me with his rubber gloves. My God, it was a bloody traumatic experience. He gave me a sheet to put over me and I covered my bloody face with it. He said, 'Mrs Baluch, I hate to tell you this, but for a husband who wasn't going to let you, you are three months pregnant.' I said, 'I can't be.'

I was absolutely distraught. Theo was sitting in the waiting room. I came out in tears, wiping my eyes with my white gloves that I wouldn't even play the organ with. He thought I had terminal cancer, naturally. He said, 'What's the matter? What's the matter?' I said, 'He told me I'm pregnant. You said I couldn't get pregnant'. He said, 'Oh, well, that's all right.' I screamed, 'What about me, what about me?' I went home and threw myself on the bed.

I was hysterical, utterly hysterical. My wedding night had been an absolute shambles. I'd never been told a bloody thing. He was a very gentle man, but at four o'clock in the morning I sat on the end of the bed and said, 'Jesus. Look I know you're there, but is this all there is to it? Is this what I'm supposed to enjoy?' And then for this dumb bastard to tell me I was pregnant and going to become a mother was all too much. Joylene, a seventeen year old on my staff, said, 'Oh, never mind, Mrs Baluch. Apples will grow again.' I said amongst tears, 'Joylene, you're sacked.' What a bloody terrible thing to say! Couldn't she think of something better to say, like sorry, instead of fucking apples? I can't even look at apples today without thinking of Joylene.

My mother finally told me about contraception after my baby was born. One night when I was chopping woodchips to feed the fire so that I could make the porridge before I went to bed, she came down to the woodheap and said, 'On the second shelf of the refrigerator there's a small packet that looks like toothpaste. They are contraceptives.' I said, 'Mum, you're ten months too bloody late.'

I sold the business, and came back to live with my parents. How could I have a baby in Adelaide with all those bloody strangers? Theo couldn't get a job as he was still that Balt bastard who'd married Joy Copley. It was really terrible for him. Michelle was born a fortnight early. It was a difficult birth and I didn't know how I was going to cope with this monkey. When I came home to my mother and father's place, I realised the situation was terribly bad between my father and Theo, so we decided to go back to Adelaide.

Michelle was three months old when we bought our house. My husband just went from one job to another. He got jobs because he looked good, but as soon as there was a threat – like writing or arithmetic – he left. He told me lies. He said he got the sack, but really he couldn't cope. I advertised to do shorthand and typing at home, but nothing came of that.

We eventually came back to Port Augusta to open a shoe shop. That was during the 1955 credit squeeze and that's when I really started to develop. I saw the acts of bastardy that are committed unless you scratch my back and I scratch yours. The incestuous bloody families that existed in Port Augusta under the name of the Chamber of Commerce had been there for generations and generations. I tried to join it. They said, 'We don't want any Balt bastards or women in the Chamber of Commerce.' I'm not a member of it to this day and never fucking intend to be. I tried to get one shop after another, but no way would they let me in. Then an arcade was built and we got a shop there. In the meantime Theo still tried to get a job but it was hopeless. They wouldn't give him standing room in the shithouse. I became more bitter and compiled a private dossier on these bloody bastards. I thought, 'If it takes me now to eternity, I'll show you bastards, I'll show you.'

From there we went into the council-built kiosk on the beach, right at the intersection of the Great Western Bridge. They called for tenders and we won that. I went in there with the £200 that was left of the lottery money. We built up a fish and chips business out of nothing. The climate was different in those days. There was no air conditioning, no television and people spent all of their time on the beach. So we had a very good turnover. Michelle used to sleep in the back of our car. She was brought up on the beach.

In order to get the lease of that kiosk I said that if they planted lawns we would water them. We nurtured and watered every blade of grass on that foreshore, every oleander and many trees, often at half past one in the morning, after working all day. There was no storeroom, and no toilet. When I asked for a toilet they charged us more. I had continuous fights with the council. I hated every council, every councillor. I said to myself, 'One day, you rotten stinken fucking bastards, I'll be calling the tune.' What really inspired me to get them were all the other people out there like me, who they were getting at. All of my bloody life people have used me, as a dog uses a post. I know what a post feels like because I've been pissed on so many times.

We introduced a juke box, a billiard table, and the first soccer machine into northern Spencer Gulf, and that's how we existed when the summer season finished. The young people of the town came there. We had our hassles with them but if they didn't behave they didn't come in, and they bloody knew it. Then the council decided to put in a swimming pool and said that our rates would have to go up. I said, 'That swimming pool is only going to provide patronage for three months of the year. What's going to happen the other nine months? I'm

I thought of the male chauvinist bloody pigs of the council . . . 'Now it's your turn, darlings . . . now you're going to fucking suffer me!'

not going to pay the rates.' So they said they'd call for tenders. I said, 'Well, you go right ahead, and when you do you'll have no bloody business.' We didn't re-tender.

With next to nothing out of the beach kiosk we went into the motel business. It was the last hotel built in Port Augusta. When people today ask me what it was before, I tell them it was a brothel. They freak out. I've never been in a brothel but I'm sure that's what they look like. The night we moved in my grandmother sat on the steps and cried. We had to live down the bad name of the previous proprietor and build that business up. Now she walks in and says, 'Look at what my granddaughter did.' My husband was still having difficulties. I thought, 'The past has been bad, the future's got to be worse.'

I was told that I could never become pregnant again. I did. And that boy is the joy of my life and his father's. Through birth trauma, he became asthmatic. He spent most of his first ten years in Escort House. If it had not been for Theo, I'm sure I would have gone mad. He is a very, very sympathetic person towards those who are sick. He used to carry that boy around for thirty-six hours on his shoulder. We would take turns, and we were still building up the business.

Then we had to face another trauma. Michelle was just eight when she was attacked in our place. I'd taken in a socially deprived person who, I later found out, had not long been out of prison and who had a long history of this behaviour. It was yet another hurdle that I had to overcome, at the same time keeping it from my parents and from everybody in our small town.

Around that time I got into local government. My son was very sick, and the Thomas Playford Power Station was emitting this shit all over Port Augusta which, according to the Public Health Department, corroded the roofs of your cars and the roofs of your houses, but did nothing to your bronchial tubes. The *Trans-Continental* wrote a beautiful editorial about that, endorsing what the Public Health Department had said. I wrote a letter back disputing it. People agreed with me, so I got a little courageous. I thought, 'Fuck you, Charlie, I've got to get in where the action is.' There were local government elections and Lyn Richies, who had been a member for Stuart and Mayor for thirty-two years, was opting out. I thought of the male chauvinist bloody pigs of the council who'd taken me to task for the withered edges of the lawns at the beach kiosk. I thought, 'Now it's your turn, darlings! I've suffered asthma, I've suffered rape, I've suffered smog, now you're going to fucking suffer me!'

As a mark of rebellion I hadn't paid rates to Port Augusta City Council for four years. So I scraped together the four years' rates in arrears, and I fronted up to the council offices with a cheque and told the Town Clerk I was going to nominate for council. He said, 'Oh, where?' I said, 'Where else but my ward?' He said, 'There's two elections there. Nesbit comes up and he's only been in there for two years, and Councillor Woodcock is contesting the mayoralty.' I said, 'I know what she's doing.' He said, 'Well she's still got one year of her term to run. Maybe it would be better if you opposed Nesbit?' I said, 'Who is opposing him?' He said, 'No one,' I said, 'Who's opposing the other?' He said, 'Five guys.' I said, 'Well, that's their bad luck because I'm going for that. So five guys and I went for that seat and I won very comfortably. People knew what I was about. They knew I was straight. I became the champion of the people who didn't know which way to go, who were under-privileged. I'll always fight for the under-dog.

I became the champion of the people who didn't know which way to go, who were under-privileged. I'll always fight for the under-dog.

I joined the Labor Party. I say to these bloody idiots here in the Labor Party today, 'You joined the Labor Party because it was trendy. I was born into it and that's the difference.' I eventually resigned because I'm so bloody disenchanted with them. Nothing could draw me back to the Labor Party. I hate their method of pre-selection. The hierarchy was really angry when I nominated for the Legislative Council. They felt threatened. I detracted a lot of votes from some of their special candidates – those they patronised in the name of the women's movement. They did me a favour because they proved to me that I've got more than they'll ever have. I've got the community behind me and they've got nothing except a bloody Party.

I was put off feminists by a lot of their sort in the Labor Party.

At a convention they will argue about a certain clause or a bloody point and they'll sit down and smoke and rave and rage. Why don't they get down to the nitty gritty? A lot of them are academics, and they really leave me cold. Let's get on with the bloody shovels and the bloody picks, and fuck the confetti.

Why don't they get down to the nitty gritty? . . . Let's get on with the bloody shovels and the bloody picks, and fuck the confetti.

I have a vision for the future of Port Augusta. Because of our geographical situation, we have to become a service centre for the great north-west hinterland. We've got Whyalla on the west and Port Pirie on the east. Port Pirie is a dying town, irrespective of what the Mayor and others say about it. The Iron Triangle Study Group Report endorsed that. Whyalla is a company town. Port Augusta is a government town. We have very little industrial unrest. My biggest concern is lack of employment for women. We have to become a major tourist centre. The tourist industry is the most labour-intensive, non-pollutant industry that one can possibly get in any community. We have the attractions of the Gulf and the Flinders Ranges and there have to be spin-offs with the introduction of the International Airport. We're three-and-a-half hours by road, and one-and-a-quarter hours by plane. And we've got a marvellous hinterland there that's just waiting to be opened. It's really an exciting time.

On an average day I get up about quarter to six and go for a swim for exercise. I shower and I'm ready to hit the deck by seven o'clock, fully made-up, dressed to greet the day. I deliver breakfasts and during the tourist season, which is fairly heavy, I cook breakfasts too. Then I have my breakfast, collect money, be nice to people, strip beds, put in washing, take loads over to the laundry, make beds, vacuum, answer the phone. The phone never stops. In between all this I see to my family. I get through all that by lunch-time. Then I have a shower, go down to the Town Hall, come back about half past five, go straight on the desk, see people in and out of the units.

Wherever I go, people say, 'I've heard a lot about you.' I say, 'Some of it's true and some of it's not.' I'll tell you a true story. One of our councillors was unable to attend this local government conference and so I had taken his dinner ticket for my husband. Before we went Theo said to me, 'I'm not going to wear Reg Baker's ticket. People know who Reg Baker is.' I said, 'Four hundred people will be there, Theo. Nobody will come up to you. As soon as you get in there take your bloody ticket off. He said, 'What will I say if they ask me what I do in local government?' I said, 'Listen, darling. If they ask you what you do in local government I'll go and piss in the nearest corner. If it happens, let me worry.' We went through the door and were introduced to various people.

Of course in every group of men, there's always a perve who sees a lone woman, even though she walks in with a group. So this one sidled up to me and cuddled up, while the father of my children was about to explode in his bloody Cossack boots and fit this bastard with a bunch of fives. He looked at Theo and said, 'Oh, and what do you do in local government?' I just stood there. Everybody else had gone, and I was left with a Cossack on my left and this bloody idiot on my right. So I had to sidle up very nonchalantly and say to him, 'He's got the hardest job in local government, in northern Spencer Gulf.' He said, 'Yeah, what's he do?' I said, 'He has to fuck the Mayor.' I was looking at him, his nose was about three inches away. He looked at me and I was steel-faced. If I'd smiled, I'd have had Cossack boots right up my backside. It was better for me to look at him, grind my back molars and not say a word. So he looked at me and thought, 'Well, right, he must be screwing her,' That shut him up, but then in came this bloke from the Highways Department. I've always introduced my husband as the father of my children and my lover. By this time Theo had left to go to the bar to refresh his glass because he'd smashed it with his fingers rather than smash it in this bastard's face. This guy from Highways said, 'Hello, darling, where's your lover?' This bastard on my right was utterly convinced that Theo had to be what I said he was. So everywhere I looked this bastard was saying, 'I don't know who he is but he's screwing the Mayor.'

It's been a long hard struggle but I love being Mayor. I'm not going to have to go on proving. I think I've shown 'em. From here on it's all down hill. It's going to be easy.

Since the first part of this interview Joy Baluch's life changed quite dramatically. She was pre-selected for the Liberal

Party for the Federal seat of Grey. Then in October 1982 she was not re-elected as Mayor of Port Augusta. Another loss followed in the March 1983 Federal election. I contacted Joy to see how this Aussie battler had coped with these two defeats.

When a high-ranking Liberal rang me and asked me to stand for pre-selection I laughed. I was convinced he'd been drinking. Finally he convinced me that the Liberals had decided that they needed somebody from the Iron Triangle cities, if they were to take the seat of Grey. They knew of my reputation in the area and that I'd resigned from the Labor Party. I'd thought about standing as an Independent but decided I couldn't afford it. I've seen how much a campaign costs. It would have nearly bloody bankrupted me. I had my vision for the northern Spencer Gulf and if the Liberals were going to back me – why not? They knew that I'd be prepared to tip the political bucket on any of them, if they didn't come up with the goods.

Port Augusta hasn't seen the last of me. Apples will grow again!

At the dinner after my pre-selection, Tony Eggleton got up and congratulated me. He said, 'I want to be in the party room when Joy Baluch tells Malcolm Fraser to get stuffed.' There were three old farmers opposite me. I'd never seen them before in my life, and one said, 'I'm going to pay my fare to go and see it.' But I never expected the antagonism that I got when my pre-selection was announced. I had nasty phone calls and unsigned letters, and people came in the night to steal my pot plants and cut down my trees. Of course there were a lot of people who still supported me as Mayor – but the ALP and the unions were out to get me. They never stopped their letters to the press saying that I couldn't do two jobs. I kept asking the press, 'How come two men had previously done both and I can't? Does having balls make all that much difference?'

When I lost the mayoralty there was such a shock reaction. A lot of people rang to say they didn't vote because they'd assumed I'd romp it in. There was only a ten per cent roll out which was much lower than the year before. I was stunned and angry, and utterly shattered to think that people didn't under-

Now I know that the higher up a woman gets and the more she tries to do things men haven't done, the more they slash away at you because of their own inadequacies.

stand that I was doing it for them. My vision was for them. I was at the annual RSL dinner when the news came. I went straight to a couple of the Labor Party and union people and gave them a serve. Then I went to my office and cleaned out every bit of paper. Two male councillors came up in tears to commiserate and help me. Of course I wept. The next day was just like the day when I'd won the mayoralty with people ringing up and coming round, except my place looked like a funeral parlour. There were so many flowers. I'm sick of sympathy.

There is never anybody at the declaration of the poll but this time there were bank managers, presidents of service clubs, and businessmen there to show their support for me. Nobody shook the incoming Mayor's hand. It was terrible. So then I thought, 'Well, I've got bigger fish to fry, and I threw myself into electioneering. When Hawke became the leader of the Labor Party I thought I'd probably had it. And I had!

Now? I'm going to open a health food shop in the main street of Port Augusta and continue to run the motel. I've got to do something with all my energy. But I'm going to hang on in there and get those bastards. I've still got a lot of support out there. I've got friends in places I didn't know I had. I'll show those bastards. My commitment to the region is even greater, if that's possible. It constitutes ninety per cent of South Australia and five generations of us have lived there.

I don't feel a failure but I do feel a bit lost now there's such an enormous gap in my life. Sometimes I feel that I've always been the right person in the right place at the wrong bloody time. I'll be fifty-one this year and I'm scared that time might run out on me. But I haven't lost my confidence or my determination. If any of my critics have the guts to criticise me face to face, I can say, 'Well, at least I've tried. What have you fucking tried to do? Shut up and piss off.' I tell you one thing – it's made me a feminist. Now I know that the higher up a woman gets, and the more she tries to do things that men haven't done, the more they slash away at you because of their own inadequacies. Sure, I'm a woman and I'm outspoken. What are you supposed to do in order to survive? At least I've blasted a trail for other women to follow. I was the first woman Mayor that Port Augusta ever had – but I wont be the last.

Port Augusta hasn't seen the last of me either. Apples will grow again!

One year later I scanned the Sunday paper for the mayoral election results. Joy Baluch had won. I rang her immediately. 'Congratulations Joy – you've done it again.' 'Thanks darling. I tell ya what, though, there's some men that had better watch out for their bloody balls.'

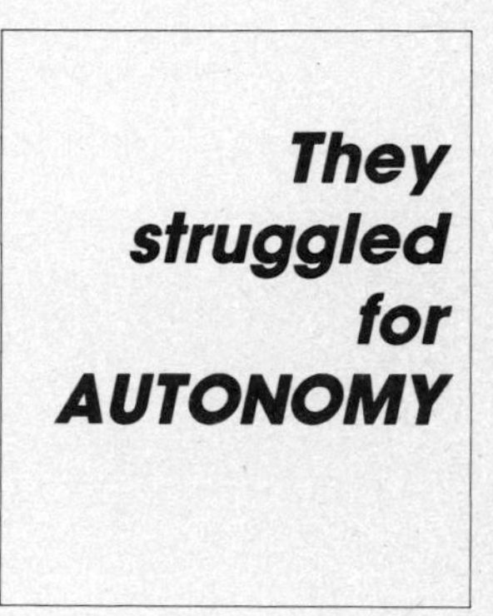
They
struggled
for
AUTONOMY

For these women, the struggle to establish themselves in their own right was paramount. In every case their sense of 'I' clashed with their sense of 'we'. They all lived with this struggle until they came to a crucial choice. They chose themselves. All of their marriages ended as a result of this choice.

When she was seventeen Maggie Tabberer's marriage to an older man established an early pattern for her as a person who did whatever her husband said. Eventually she made a stand and said 'No', and began to state her own needs and demands. She continued to assert herself and her independence knowing the marriage would end, and started alone to build a successful career for herself and her children.

Pat Lovell tried so hard to fulfil firstly her parents' needs and then her husband's that eventually she experienced a total loss of self. She realised that in order to be the person she really was she would have to stop trying to salvage the marriage. Having acted on that decision she threw herself into her work and discovered her strengths and talents.

Pat O'Shane had to struggle not only with the problems of being a woman in a sexist society but also with the problems of being an Aboriginal in a racist one. The tension within her marriage accelerated her breakdown. She went to Sydney alone to confront the horrors of mental illness. Having overcome this she decided to end the marriage and study law. She became Australia's first Aboriginal lawyer and has never lost the strength she gained from that decision.

MAGGIE TABBERER (Fashion designer, consultant and journalist)

'I'll be in Melbourne for the Logies. Ring me early the morning after.'

At nine o'clock I tentatively dialled Maggie's room number in the hotel. I had watched the Logie Awards in my hotel room and they were more like a marathon race than an entertainment. I had fallen asleep at one-thirty and they were still going. The bright voice on the other end of the phone said, 'Come on up and have some breakfast. I feel great.'

As I rode up in the lift, I remembered coming home at lunch-time from university (a long time ago) and watching the beautiful Maggie on *Beauty and the Beast*. And here I was wearing my 'Maggie T' outfit and hoping my make-up was in place.

She opened the door and the face I saw was fresh and alert and practically free of make-up. Unlike Maggie, I'm not an early morning person. Perhaps it's time I changed my habits.

If you had to classify me, I'd say, 'Put me down as a worker.' I've always worked.

At school all I did was get into trouble. I was a dreamer and a hopeless student. I was fairly good at sport and art, but I was especially good at getting into trouble for talking too much. I was a chatterbox and never shut up.

Just recently in Adelaide an unknown face out of the crowd came up to me and said, 'I went to school with you.' I said, 'Did you really?' She said, 'Yes, my name is so-and-so.' I couldn't

quite remember her. She had kept in touch with a lot of girls who were either in my class or the class below and she told me how they were all so stunned about my success because they always thought that I was such a ding-a-ling in school. They couldn't believe I could have done what I have. I guess I'm as surprised as them. I really was hopeless. I thought school was terribly boring. I always wanted to be out climbing trees and playing with the chaps. I was a terrible tomboy.

Also, about a year and a half ago, this tall guy walked towards me at the races in Adelaide and said, 'You'll never remember me.' I said, 'You're Tarzan.' He used to be Tarzan and I was Jane. After watching the Tarzan and Jane movies at the Saturday matinées, we'd swing on ropes hung from a huge tree in the vacant allotment on the corner of our street. He said, 'I should have known that you were going to do something with your life.' I said, 'How is that?' And he said, 'Well, you were so aggressive. I remember one occasion we'd been to the movies and we'd seen Tarzan struggle with this huge lion, so we went to re-enact this under the tree. I jumped down and fought off this imaginary lion and did this whole number. Then I looked up to you for approval whereupon you said scornfully, "Well, kill it!"' He said, 'I think that is very significant.'

I loved Girl Guides because I loved the camping and that sort of outdoorsy thing. I'm also a Sagittarian and they are supposed to love being outdoors. I like that sort of freedom. Even very early on I used to play hookey. Actually in that period the school system was probably pretty boring. I was born in 1936 and my schooling was in the '40s.

I'm an aggressive person. I was the youngest of a large family and I fought like cat and dog with my brothers and sister. I love them now but they gave me a hard time as a child, as always happens in large families. Mother will ask the eldest daughter to wipe up, and she'll tell the next one, and she'll tell the next one, etc. I was always the bottom of the queue. I had a lot of arguments. My mother and I had a very good relationship and I adored my dad. He was rather beautiful, a gorgeous man, but he drank too much. Mother was the strong one. She was the one who whacked you when you misbehaved. She made the family decisions.

I'm not someone who thinks about the past. I'm so busy thinking about what I'm going to do today.

I wasn't aware of the value of my looks until I met Helmut Newton, the famous photographer. I used to think that I was funny-looking. My sister Nancy was the beautiful one in the family. Everyone said so. I adored her. I was longer and thinner and more angular. I was so much taller than everybody else and all arms and legs.

I'm an honest person. I say what I feel and what I think. Eric Baume, the 'Beast' on *Beauty and the Beast*, taught me a good lesson when I first began in television. He said, 'You'd better be honest, kid, because they're going to catch you out if they think you're not telling them the truth.' That was very good advice. But I told terrible fibs as a kid, like saying that we lived in a big house or that my father was a policeman. I had wonderful fantasies. I used to make up marvellous stories and tell people that these dramatic things had happened to me. I suppose it was a form of escapism. I was very conscious of my background. Now when I go to posh parties back in Adelaide I sometimes laugh a bit inside and think, 'All these people don't know that I'm really little Margaret Tregar from Parkside.' In the old days you never admitted you came from Parkside because that's where the funny-farm was. People used to make terribly rude comments about that, so you immediately removed yourself to the other side of the tramline and said you came from Unley. I went to Unley Primary and then on to the technical school there.

When I left school at fourteen I worked in a pharmacy until my sister, a hairdresser, could con her boss into taking me on as a junior. For six months I scrubbed heads in a small salon in Gawler Place in Adelaide. I hated it. My best girlfriend told me of a vacancy for an accountant machinist in the office where she worked. I knew nothing about accounting, and I still can't add up my cheque book! Somehow, though, I got the job and hung in there for a year. I hated that too, so I thought I'd get married and have babies. Being the youngest of a large family, my parents were quite weary by then, especially as I hadn't been a very well-behaved child. I thought it would be easier to do what I wanted with a husband who adored me, rather than with two parents. I got married for the reason that most young girls at that age think they want to get married – a knight in shining white armour. In this instance it was a very dashing man twenty years older than me and a white Chevrolet convertible. In those years everyone married young. All my sisters had married young. It seemed to be the conventional thing to do.

I always felt that I came from the wrong side of the tracks. But there is a strong class thing in Adelaide. When I first met my first husband, Charles Tabberer, he was a member of the Keswick and Wayville tennis club, and played golf and did all those sort of things. I didn't come from that class at all. I met him at a boyfriend's birthday party held at Charles' house in North Adelaide. He didn't attend the party but he came home later. He asked to be introduced to me and that was that. It was a whirlwind affair. Three months later we were engaged and three months after that we were married. I was seventeen and very much in love. My parents were so relieved to get rid of me. He could have been 2 000 years old and they would have said, 'Let her go, for God's sake, let's get rid of her. Thank God she's gone.' Let's face it, he was better-off than the average, and they thought that he was quite a good catch. And so did I, because he had a lovely house as well as this big white car.

He'd say, 'We're going to do this,' and, 'We're going to do that,' And I always did what I was told. One day I just said, 'I think I won't do that.'

Anyway, he belonged to this bloody tennis club of Keswick and Wayville and unless you were a club member you were not allowed in the club house – the club house being this incredible tin shack, I might add. God knows why it was so snobby. Anyway, he used to take his former lady there. He had convinced the committee that he was definitely going to marry her, so she was allowed into the club house. But he didn't marry her and when he tried to pull the same act with me they said, 'Oh, no.' So I had to sit out on this rotten little bench while he went in and ordered a drink after the match. Right up until we were married I wasn't allowed to go in. I was furious, but I put up with it. What was I going to do? I was mad about him. If he said we were going to play tennis, we played tennis. Eventually, that caused the breakdown of the marriage. He was a very strong man. Being that much older he always told me what to do. He'd say, 'We're going to do this,' and, 'We're going to do that.' And I always did what I was told. One day I just said, 'I think I won't do that.' That's when the rot set in. By then I had two children. As a mother you grow up pretty rapidly – it doesn't matter how young you are.

It was on a trip to Melbourne early in my marriage that I met Helmut Newton – the legendary Newton. I was so scared. A friend took me to a funny little studio in Flinders Lane, and there was the master. He said, 'Yes, I'm very interested in photographing you.' I went back to Adelaide thinking how nice it had all been. About a week later I got a phone call asking me to go to Melbourne and do a job for the Pierre Cardin newsletter. So I big-adventured, dumped the kids with Mum, packed my bags and jumped on an aeroplane. I earned an unbelievable sum of money and went back to Adelaide. A week later there was another phone call. It quickly became apparent that in fact I had the means of earning some decent dough, so Charles and I decided to move. I worked there for two years. Charles didn't mind my working. Most men don't mind their wives working, because of the extra money.

My husband actually left me. I must honestly say I didn't try to stop him. By then I felt that the marriage had run its course. My heart does a contraction when I think about it now. I must have been really stupid and naïve because I was so young. If you think about the awesome task of bringing up two children by yourself when you haven't been educated to have any sort of career, or even a job, it's frightening. But I was making decent money modelling at the time so I thought I'd just flop along doing that and everything would be all right. A young girl lived with me and looked after the kids. Even though I was earning good dough, it wasn't easy being a single parent, hiring someone to look after the kids, worrying about their schooling, and there were a lot of difficult years.

I felt I needed a man around to protect me. My parents were not in a situation to help me. My mother was one of those ramrod women who said, 'You've made your bed, now you lie on it.' It would never have occurred to me to do what a lot of girls obviously are forced to do – and I don't say this unkindly – to pack up the kids and go home. When my marriage ended, I didn't feel a failure. He had failed. I hadn't. I wasn't devastated, because it hadn't been nice living like that. He was unhappy and we were making the kids unhappy. I do remember the pain when he had finally gone. The moment it does

I did expect my husband to help financially in the early stages but it wasn't to be. I thought, 'Right, I'll do it by myself.'

happen, you get this incredible feeling of loneliness and anguish. Really, for quite a long time I wondered if I had done the right thing. But if it had to break up, it was better then, when they were such babies.

Their father didn't see them a lot afterwards. It's a terrible thing to say, but I think that also helps. The children are not torn and you don't have all that confrontation. I did expect my husband to help financially in the early stages but it wasn't to be. I thought, 'Right, I'll do it by myself. If he doesn't help pay for the kids he hasn't any right to come around.' I was bitter that neither he, his mother nor any of his relations ever rang to ask if they could help. Never. They might say they thought that was what I wanted. Perhaps I did, I don't know. Eventually, I came to terms with it and thought, 'Oh well, it's an easier way for me,' and I didn't push for maintenance at all.

Two years later Helmut took off for Europe and wanted me to go, but I couldn't drag two little children of three and four off to Europe and work. It seemed too hard. I went to live in Sydney. That was when I started the battle of the bulge. I don't know whether that came about through some sort of anxiety. Inside I really knew that modelling was a pretty short-term career. So, unconsciously, I put on weight and was forced to do something else. But I'm not someone who sits down and thinks about the past. I'm so busy thinking about what am I going to do today. It's very hard for me to recall those traumatic times. I do remember not knowing where I was going to get the money to pay the rent.

But I'd met Ettore by then and, even though our relationship was on and off, I knew that he was there if I really needed help. He was a strong man and he adored the children, which was marvellous. Even when he and I were having our off-periods, he and the kids were always doing very well together. I was absolutely mad about him. He was another knight on a white charger. I'm designed that way. If I do fall in love, I fall boots and all. No half-measures for me. I wanted to spend the rest of my life with him, but he wasn't going to be caught for a long time. He'd been married before and wasn't into getting married again. He thought we could just go on the way we were.

It nearly killed my mother when I confessed to her that I was living with Ettore. I came from the sort of background where you just didn't do that, but you didn't lie to a woman like my mother. She used to worry herself sick about me of course, so it was a good thing that she lived in Adelaide and I lived in Sydney. She would have been mortified seeing me struggling with day-to-day things. Occasionally she would come over and say, 'You can't go on like this.' And whilst she didn't ask me to live at home with her again, she thought I should at least return to Adelaide and get out of sin city. 'Not a place to bring up children, Margaret,' she used to say.

I really never felt guilty about not being a 'proper' mother either. There weren't any options. If the children were to have a roof over their heads . . . I had to work.

So I was still a single mother living in Sydney. I drifted out of modelling, and into other areas of the fashion industry. I worked for designer Hal Ladlow, a great chum of mine who needed someone in the showroom. I arranged his showings, saw his clients and kept him to his deadlines. Helmut had taught me a lot. I also worked a great deal for *Vogue* (Australia) and Bernard Laser, the head of *Vogue*, became a great chum too. He told me, 'Maggie, you've got to do something more than hang around modelling.' I knew in my heart that I had to get out of modelling before they got me out. Dieting was a constant struggle. I remember Georges, Melbourne's top store, flying me down to Melbourne to do their parades. I'd always done their big showings. But when I got there I didn't fit the clothes. I stumbled out into the street and burst into tears. They just couldn't use me for the show. I caught the plane back to Sydney feeling absolutely devastated. I knew I had to do something else.

Bernard Laser said, 'Why don't you get into the promotion side?' I said, 'I don't know anything about that.' He said, 'You'll learn, you'll be all right.' He got me my first account with a chemical company. I promoted a fibre of theirs called Lurex. All the people I'd worked for as a model were the contacts and I started to move into commercial business. I didn't believe that I could do it, but I had to try something else. It was necessity. It's always been necessity. I had to earn a living to look after my kids. So I started at home with a little typewriter. I'd take the kids to school, come home, get dressed, run out and do my job, pick them up at three o'clock and go home and type my own letters. Then some idiot offered me a second account and I had to get a couple of telephones and open an office. That's how I began.

About the same time I went on the panel of Channel Seven's show, *Beauty and the Beast*. At that stage I think they were just looking for reasonably attractive, fairly well-known dames, and I had had a fair bit of publicity. Yes, I admit that my looks have opened quite a few doors. Eric Baume loved all of us and treated us as family, particularly the original girls. He made me cry once on camera. He came backstage afterwards and said, 'You silly old bitch, what's the matter with you?' But he was really saying sorry. I am a bit of a cryer. I see little old ladies trying to get on trams and I cry, I go and see movies and I cry. I'm sentimental about soppy, silly things. I know I don't look it. People think I'm such a tough bitch, but I really am not. I'm not a stewer either, especially in terms of having arguments. That's probably a good thing. In my family environment you would not have had time to stew. We were always rolling out of one argument into another as kids. The Fighting Tregars we might have been known as. Conflict doesn't worry me, but I like to be liked.

I remember when *The Maggie Show* was in its final stages, the head of Channel Seven said to me, 'You really shouldn't stay in television, you're not tough enough.' I said, 'What do you mean? I think I'm fairly tough.' He said, 'No, you like to be liked by too many people. You can't accept not being liked and in this industry you have to.' He could well have been right. As it was, I felt my television days had come to an end anyway. I had had eight good years and again it was time to do something else.

I made some good chums on *Beauty and the Beast*. Last night I saw Hazel Phillips from the panel at the presentation of the Logies and that was wonderful. We had been in the same situation, as she had two boys to bring up. Those days we used to get the odd letter of criticism saying, 'What about those old bags sitting up there on *Beauty and the Beast*? How can they give all this advice?' I remember Eric saying, 'Maggie Tabberer is divorced, Pat Lovell is separated and Hazel Phillips is divorced, so how can they be telling other women?' And of course, we ripped into him on camera the next day and said, 'We can offer advice because we've been through it.' I think that helped make the show successful in the early days. It's a dead format now. It's not applicable today for a viewer to say, 'My nineteen-year-old daughter came in at two o'clock in the morning, what am I going to do?' She's lucky she's still living at home. It's so dated. Being on the show could sometimes be a bit frightening. People would enter into long correspondence with you about their lives and sometimes they were mentally disturbed. A show like that always attracts a certain type of person. But I liked being on television. Before I remarried it was also a living. I used to record at the weekend which gave me enough money to pay the rent and feed the children.

When I was on *Beauty and the Beast* I got a message at the station to ring Zel Rabin, the editor of the *Daily Mirror*. I was going through my divorce at the time and all I could envisage were glaring headlines in the *Mirror*, like, 'Beauty divorced', or something equally awful. When I finally got up the courage to ring him, this slow voice said, 'I want to talk to you about doing a column.' When I went to see him he said, 'Can you write like you talk?' I said, 'I can't even spell. I don't even know where to put the commas.' He said, 'Write it how you'd say it.' He'd been at home sick and had seen me on the panel. So that's how I became a fashion columnist. I stuck faithfully to Zel's words of wisdom, which were 'Keep it light, tight and bright. Don't use words that you don't understand, the chance is no one else will understand them either.' I was with the *Mirror* for sixteen years.

I married the second time in 1968. After marriage I went on with my own career except for a time when I was pregnant, though even then I still worked on *Beauty and the Beast* as I could sit behind a desk without worrying how big I got. After I lost the baby I only took off about three or four months. It was the most traumatic thing losing the baby. It was a year before I could go to sleep. Just dreadful. I still get emotional about it. I'm sorry . . .

My big hang-up is the fact that I am not educated. I was determined that my children should have the best education. I had to keep working to keep them at school. Of course, they're exactly like me. Brooke hated school and couldn't wait to get out. She is a toughie and at seventeen she just said, 'Look no way. You're trying to make me do something because you didn't. I'm not going to do that.' Amanda complied a bit longer and took herself off to university but she only lasted six months. She came home and said, 'I can't stand it, I'm not cut out for it. I don't feel I am achieving anything. For Christ's sake, let me go to work and start to earn my way in life.' I suddenly realised that I had given birth to two that were just like me. It does worry me really deep down. I've never got over the feeling that I wasn't very bright. It doesn't matter how much I achieve or how well I do something.

Amanda and I were talking recently about something I'm involved in, and she said, 'You're just getting bored with it, because it's like everything you do. You throw yourself into it, you tackle it with vengeance, you conquer it in six months or a year and then you don't want to know about it.' I thought suddenly, 'Am I really like that?' And I suppose I am. Then she said, 'What about some of the things you've pulled off?' And she listed them. I never sit down and think about them. I don't say, 'Okay, I'm not really educated, but I should feel proud of myself because I did this and this and this . . .' It's only when I talk to someone about my life that I start to think, 'Oh yes, I did do that, that was pretty good.' I know I shouldn't, but I really think I'll carry that hang-up to my grave. But I'm not going back to knock off an Arts degree, oh Jesus, no. I hated school and I'd hate it now.

I'm always slightly surprised at my success, and that I've done all those things. Amanda has a clearer picture of me. She pointed out that, despite the fact that I didn't have an education and wasn't prepared or equipped to go out in the world, I did carve a career: I modelled and won the award as the top model in Australia; I went into television, became the top woman in television and won two Gold Logies; I went into the publicity business and I worked some of the best accounts in the field of fashion and beauty; I staged the fashion awards, which is the ultimate. These are the sort of things she says I should count. I'm street-wise, not educated. I've got nous, I'm very practical and can organise myself and other people. That dates back to being part of a big family when you had to do those things.

When you reach the top you get nervous about staying

there. That's the worry. There are some things in my life that I would like to discard, but my pride won't let me. At the moment I think I'd like to do something totally different. Barbara Turnbull, my closest friend in life, is very creative and artistic. We have vacations together occasionally, and I draw and paint. She thinks it's terrible that I don't use that talent, and I know she is right. That will be the next thing I'll do. I want to design fabrics and marvellous prints, so there will be 'Maggie T' sheets and things like that. It's all tied in with the fashion life-style. But that's still a bit up the track. I'm not finished with this yet.

You know I'd still worry about not earning a dollar, even if I was a multi-millionaire. I remember having my bum beaten because I raided the larder and whacked off a quarter of a pound of butter on a piece of bread. My mother almost burst into tears because I had obliterated what was to be enough butter for dinner for five. It was really rough. But I'm not careful with money, I'm generous with it. In fact, it's one of the things Ettore and I argue about. I say, 'Stuff it, I'm not going to sit around and stash all this dough away so when I'm sixty-five I can go around the world first-class. Bugger that, I want to do it now.' And I do. I enjoy travelling first-class, staying in the best hotels, buying myself a pair of $150 shoes if I really want to. I enjoy the money that I'm earning. Anyway, with my luck, if I stashed it away, the day they said, 'You can stop worrying Mag, you've got enough money in the bank,' I'd walk out the bloody front door and get knocked over by a bus.

My life's been full of highs and lows. But I'd rather have it like that than have every day the same. I just couldn't cope. I tackle so many things sometimes that I terrify myself. It's as if somebody is kicking me and saying, 'You've got to do it.' I woke up one morning when Ettore was overseas and I was bored. There wasn't anybody around to have an argument with. I was lying there thinking, 'Oh, I have a headache and a leg-ache, I'm probably going to have an early menopause,' but I decided, 'No, I'd better not do that. What'll I do? I'll buy a boat.' I find that a very strange train of thought – no, I will not have a menopause, I'll buy a boat instead. When Ettore came home I said, 'I want to buy a boat.' He said, 'That'll be nice,' thinking I just wanted a little speedboat. I said, 'No, actually, something a bit bigger.' I bought myself this whacking great, brand new, twenty-five foot Bertram. Then I had to learn to drive it. I can now. It's fantastic and I'm on the boat every minute that I can. It's one of the things I feel that I have conquered. It's curious – I talk about that as an achievement and yet I don't talk about the work things as an achievement.

As a general rule I don't work after office hours. I'm a very early riser. A lot of people think I am a workaholic, but what else would I do? I couldn't sit around at home. The only time I haven't worked was when I was ill. I've had a lot of illness. In my thirties, everybody had Christmas and I had an operation. It's true. I had something like four bladder operations, a gall stone operation and then a Caesarian. Every year I was in hospital. I'm really very lucky to be as fit as I am now. I have been very healthy for the last ten years. I just don't believe now that I'm going to get sick.

So we both live very individual lives but together lives at the same time. I reckon we have the best of both worlds. You are yourself and yet you're a partner at the same time.

Ettore and I are still together, after something like twenty-two years. Sometimes we get on better than at other times. I don't endorse dishonesty, but I think there are things in relationships that are better not spoken about. If you want to retain a good relationship I think you should exercise a bit of tact and discretion. I am so jealous, I'd kill. It's better if I don't know. I have been known to react rather violently. I've attacked him and the other woman in my time. And he has behaved in exactly the same way. His behaviour can be very Italian, though he is most generous in tolerating my life-style. I mean, I'm in Melbourne two days a week and when I'm back in Sydney I might be out two nights a week. I hardly conform to the good wife who's there cooking meals. Mind you, we still have big family lunches and spend our weekends together. But he has never ever said, 'You can't.' He'd be in trouble if he did. He sometimes tells me, 'Maggie, you're too strong a woman.'

We have three sets of friends. He has a lot of close Italian friends and they have card-playing, Italian sort of nights. I play cards, but that's not how I see myself spending an evening, even if I stay home. It's never expected that I go. And likewise, because of the work I'm in, a lot of my friends are homosexual. I really enjoy their company, but I know Ettore doesn't want to do that night after night either. So we both live very individual lives but together lives at the same time. I reckon we have the best of both worlds. You are yourself and yet you're a partner at the same time. I consider myself very lucky to be able to have that. He's never taken on that traditional Italian male role, probably because I had already established my own identity as Maggie Tabberer when we finally married. He isn't threatened by my fame, though he might be a little bit sick of it at times. He doesn't like to be called Mr Tabberer, which happens occasionally.

I've only once been denied something because I was a woman. It was during my television career. My experience with the network was well-rounded and a night show was coming up. I was perfectly capable of sitting in that chair and doing a damn good job. I knew it and they knew it, but I didn't get it because I was a woman. An executive said to me, 'We don't believe that the Australian public wants to sit down at night and watch a woman host a tonight show.' And I said, 'Oh, shit.' That might have been one of the reasons why I thought that I couldn't go any further in television. I didn't want to be locked into daytime television, because they wouldn't let me on at night. So I thought, 'Stuff it.' I was also tired of that whole network syndrome thing that I was going through then. They had moved my time-slot because they'd sold a bigger programme on a national basis. Once they start to mess your programme around like that, your ratings drop and you can only go down. So I walked out while I still had a good image in the industry. They told me to have a nice holiday and gave me a ticket to go around the world. Of course that took me out of circulation while the other networks were putting together programmes for the ongoing year. By the time I came back everybody's programming was locked in for the next year.

But I'm not strong in the area of sexual discrimination. I haven't really analysed it. I've had some bad experiences with the women's movement. I went back to Adelaide to open an art exhibition during International Women's Year, 1975. I stood up and made a light-hearted opening speech with some reference to liking men, or something. And these three very butch ladies came up and practically ripped my arms off and said that I had set the women's movement back twenty years. I was furious and told them to fuck off. I looked at them and thought, 'You say you're going to advance women, but look how you go about it.' I haven't read *The Female Eunuch* or any of those books. It really hasn't touched me much. I believe

It's all a question of individual rights and choice. If that's what you want to do then go and do it.

women have a right to do all those things. It's all a question of individual rights and choice. If that is what you want to do, then go and do it, unless you're stopped, of course. As I was stopped from doing my tonight show. But women will get there if they want to. Or they'll do something else. It's up to the individual. At times I'm probably seen as a bit of a traitor to my sex because I haven't been involved in the women's movement. I always give the same answer, 'If they want to do that, they should go out and do it themselves. They shouldn't try and make me feel guilty about not doing it.'

I really never felt guilty about not being a 'proper' mother either. There weren't any other options. If the children were to have a roof over their heads, if they were to have good food and be able to go to riding camp and have an education, I had to work. It's silly to sit there and wallow in that sort of guilt. I certainly didn't. A lot of women are made to feel guilty, but what alternative is there? Even if you didn't have kids but needed to go out and work for yourself, you should have the right to do it. That's what I mean by saying, 'Everybody is inside their own skin, they've got to do what they've got to do.' If other women don't want to work or don't need to work, that's their avenue in life. They shouldn't feel guilty about wanting to be a housewife. Women are better organisers and often more practical than men. We would be better managers of the world if given an opportunity.

I think that I am a role-model for women. It's great when someone says, 'I sat at home and my marriage broke up. Then when I was watching you on television, I thought, "Well, you did it. So I got off my bum and did it too."' Now, with the 'Maggie T' clothes, women say, 'I don't have to be Twiggy. Now I can put something decent on and I feel terrific. I can't thank you enough, you've changed my life.' They're nice things.

Getting chubby was a good way to begin making clothes for chubby ladies. I was able to dress reasonably well because friends in the industry would make me special things during those 'getting bigger' years, or I would have my clothes made by a dressmaker. Several years before I'd made 'Maggie Tabberer for Big Girls' with a manufacturer. The range was tremendously successful the first season but the second season there were production problems with quality and the cut and things. I knew that unless I was going to be a hundred per cent involved that it was really not going to operate well. I decided that it was better not to continue. Then masses of women wrote complaining that I'd stopped making them. So I knew there was a very positive market out there.

Four years later, Carl Dowd of the Clothing Company came to me with some figures. He'd actually researched the market and he knew that thirty per cent of women in Australia are a size fourteen and another thirty per cent are above that. That's sixty per cent of the population. We're a majority group, being treated like a minority. I liked him very much and I felt that we could have a good working relationship. We sorted out the dollars and launched 'Maggie T'. It's really engaging and I enjoy it enormously, though it takes up an enormous amount of my time and involves a lot of travel. I am involved on a consultancy basis and also on the sales and promotion side.

I really get a kick out of seeing people look good in my clothes. I think we all hate the fat on ourselves a little. But of course you feel better if you can wear the right clothes. You can cover it all up. I suppose I've been lucky because my problems are from my boobs to my crutch. I can cover up all the fat. My legs and my arms are thinner. But I get women coming up to me in the street and saying, 'I love your clothes, but when are you going to make them for short women?' And I say, 'When you become the majority, because we make clothes for the average height.' I also get a certain group of women saying, 'I never see anything like you wear. Why can't I get that in the range?' It's hard to please all the people all the time. One day at the airport I thought this short lady was going to kick me right in the kneecap. She really went off her trolley. She was about four feet nine tall and wide. I said to her, 'Do you realise that Margaret Whitlam complains to me that we don't leave enough material for her to let the hems down?'

I'm also working on the *Women's Weekly* as fashion editor, which again is a lot of work. I like it, but I hate being restricted to eight pages at a time. I think they should give me twenty pages. Dawn Swain, the editor, is a really good woman. She is not as visible as Ita Buttrose was. She doesn't want to be an up-front lady, but she has done a phenomenal job with the magazine.

And then there is Maggie Tabberer Associates, the public relations business which Amanda is involved in. Jan Leavy has been a marvellous partner for the past fifteen years. I do the creative side and she does all the accounts and administration. I'm very much involved in the big shows. I design the sets and the lighting and work with really top people. The whole shape of the thing becomes my baby, and I love that. I'm also engaged by the Nine Network to host six Mike Walsh shows a year while Mike is away having his well-deserved breaks.

I'm a fairly optimistic person . . . If everything that I'm involved in now suddenly fell away, I know I would cope because I've coped before.

Things open and shut for me. I sense times of change and that a door in my life is going to open. I make commitments quickly because if I sit around and think about them I'll duck out. So usually I over-commit myself and then I have to measure up. Women are intuitive and have an innate sensitivity. Every woman knows within her own gut that she has had a feeling about something but she hasn't listened. We've all gone through an experience we've regretted. I do listen to that inner voice. That's part of what I call being streetwise.

I've always been clever enough to surround myself with the best in whatever field I'm working in. Those people who get threatened by other people's talent are crazy. Good people make you look good. As to failures – I don't look back. I don't sit around saying, 'In 1978 . . .' I can't even remember bloody dates. I really don't live life back there. I am a fairly optimistic person. If suddenly I did something scandalous or if everything that I'm involved in now fell away, I know I would cope because I coped before. If I have to scrub kitchen floors, I'll be the best scrubber of kitchen floors. I really don't have any fear about that. I like making a dollar and I like being what Maggie Tabberer is about. But it won't hang me up if it falls away from me tomorrow.

I'm confident in our marriage. I'm not afraid of getting old. I'm a bit frightened of death. Just basically scared. Probably a little bit of a religious hang-up there, I think. If you're good you go up, and if you're bad you go down. The old Baptist notion of sin is still with me. There is a lot of early Adelaide in me. Sometimes I really get cross with myself about that. I wish I could cast that off, but I can't. I'm still the little girl from Parkside trying to prove that I can do it. I hope one day I'll be able to say, 'Stuff it,' and draw those orchids on sheets or something.

Just before I left Maggie said, 'When you go back and put all this together will you tell me what you really think of me? Will you ring me up and tell me who I am? I can't really analyse it. I'm still slightly surprised that I'm me. People often say, "If you had a dozen words to describe yourself to the rest of the world, what would you say?" It absolutely throws me. I can't do it.'

Now you have read the interview you will be able to give Maggie the dozen words she needs. See how they match with mine: warm; generous; gutsy; modest; perceptive; imaginative; practical; energetic; witty; intelligent; spontaneous; and above all, unpretentious.

PAT LOVELL (Film producer)

We sat opposite each other in canvas steamer chairs. The room was furnished simply. The walls displayed posters of Pat's previous films. There was none of that Hollywood show-biz, 'Take a seat, dahling. I'll be with you in a minute.' No-nonsense, straight, and yet a manner that was a bit aloof. Or was it shy? A willingness to talk about her life and yet a defensiveness that was almost tangible. She said she hadn't slept much the night before. Too many things on her mind. At three in the morning she had turned on the light and read Dirk Bogarde's autobiography. His childhood world was a lot like hers.

I was always really keen about marriage and being a family person. Even though I'm an individualist, I do like to be part of something. I loved my husband very dearly. He'd had a pretty upsetting time because his first wife had died and he had a daughter. So I started behind the eight ball because I married into endless problems. I thought I was strong enough to cope. It was a challenge. I thought if you loved somebody deeply enough you could overcome everything. And I really did try very hard for a long time. But love doesn't conquer all! It really doesn't.

One of the reasons that the marriage lasted for as long as thirteen years was the fact that I was constantly being reminded by my husband that after all I had come from a broken family and was unstable. He was an actor and had a hell of a lot of problems. Looking back on it now I suppose I didn't give him as much time as I should have because I had a step-daughter and two small kids within three years of marriage. We lived out of the city, which I still do, as I love it, but it rather kept him away because he would go to the city to work, then go off and have drinks with the boys. I'd be lucky to see him for dinner. More often than not his dinner would be on a saucepan with a lid over it. The night before my daughter was born he told me that he felt we were ill-matched from the start. We'd only been married a year so it was a pretty devastating thing to hear. I disagreed with him then but looking back on it, I think he was right.

Possibly the best thing that I ever did, even though it was a horrendous thing to do at the time, was to walk out on him. It did not endear me to anybody, I can assure you. I don't think anybody realises how difficult it is to do that. You have to be beyond words to do it. Utterly desperate. People have said to me, 'Oh, we think we're going to separate but we'll get Christmas over first.' That to me is just ridiculous. If you really feel it, you can't be that civilised. I had got to the stage where I knew that I was in for a big breakdown because there was no way I could lead a sort of double life. My husband at that stage felt that we could cohabit but have friends elsewhere, and to me that just doesn't work at all. I think you're either in it or you're not.

Possibly the best thing I ever did, even though it was horrendous at the time, was to walk out on him . . . You have to be beyond words to do that. Utterly desperate.

I could see that my stress was telling on the kids. It was a painful decision to make especially as I still liked him. But it was because I still liked and respected him that I had to do it. I could see that we were getting to the stage where the name-calling and the horror was about to start. We would have become like a pair of frightful animals if we kept up that sort of behaviour. It was absolutely inevitable because over the thirteen years it had got steadily worse and worse and worse. We'd hardly been communicating for years.

I'd chosen the worst time of the year – December – to move out of a household. Annie Deveson came to my aid. She and her husband were moving out of a house that they hadn't resold, so I had a temporary residence to go to. My other good friend rallied around and lent me an old washing machine and an old fridge and things like that, but I literally did pack up and leave. The day after, I felt an immense weight off my mind. I realised that for the past three years I had been living in some sort of terrible nightmare. I had told both the children that we were going and Jenny had just hugged me and said, 'I'm so glad.' She was eleven and Sam was nine. He became the man of the house extremely quickly and was a great stalwart to me regardless of being so young. I don't put the blame anywhere. I just knew it was an untenable situation and said, 'Bear with me – I've got to give it a go.' Initially I thought it would be a temporary arrangement until I got my head together. Then I realised that it couldn't be temporary because the person that I was forced to be within that marriage was just not me. I had not been myself for too long.

My husband was able to see the kids any time he wished. There was no problem there. Naturally he was terribly upset and did try to convince them that the separation was not a good idea, but we seemed to get through that difficult time. Even though we've kept separate households I don't think they've ever lost each other. They are all very close, and now my son and daughter are both away from home they see him almost as much as they see me, which is good. He and I are always together when they need us. When my son graduated I was there with him. When my daughter graduated unfortunately I was overseas, but my husband was there with my mother and some good friends.

He hasn't remarried and neither have I. I don't think I will. I'd make a rotten wife for anybody now, particularly in the business I'm in. I do literally have to give everything to it. I'd drive any guy bananas because apart from my children it is my whole life. I did look around initially thinking I'd like to get married again, or live with somebody. It's important to have a really good relationship with a man. But nobody appeared who wanted to work at it as much as I did. I sometimes worry about it. It would be much more fun to be with a guy. But I guess it's the luck of the draw really. I've never met anybody with whom I'd really want to share the life I've built up. Or vice versa. It's a two-way thing.

I definitely think there are scars from my childhood that I will never lose, because it was filled with a great deal of sadness. I'm one of three surviving children out of six. My childhood was dogged by death. My elder brother died two days after I was born, which left an indelible scar on my mother. I don't think she ever realised how it also fell on to my shoulders. My father did, and over-compensated by spoiling me a lot. Then my younger brother died. Fortunately my next brother survived and he's a great guy. Then I had another sister who is eleven years younger than me and she's hale and hearty. But eighteen months after she was born, my mother had another daughter who had a hole in the heart and she died too. My mother really had a hell of a life, just to put it mildly. But she was marvellous when we were small. She created a magic world for us in our western suburbs' backyard with its two plum trees, a persimmon tree, a big sandpit and a little pond. I lived in an absolute fantasy world within that garden.

I consciously tried to cut out the pain when I was little. We were on a train when my mother told me about my younger brother's death. I'd been staying with friends. I remember being absolutely shattered and wanting to bawl my eyes out. But I thought it wouldn't be right to do that, not on public transport. Grief is something you hide. So I probably made some smart remark because that's always been my way of coping. I still do it. It's a very bad way of getting over deep emotion. I know my mother wrote to an aunt soon afterwards saying I was a fairly unfeeling person. I wasn't. I was trying to hide. I didn't want to distress her any more by bawling or making a scene . . . I still get very upset when I think about it. She didn't understand.

Very early I found another world that was tenable when my own was untenable. I was always making up plays and performing them. I even had the gall to charge my parents to come. My father put on the best kids' parties I've ever come across in my life. Later I tried to reconstruct the same things for my children. They were wonderful parents in that there was lots of fun. My mother used to read to us a lot. We were brought up on *The Jungle Book* by Rudyard Kipling. When Peter Weir was directing *Gallipoli* and asked for that piece from *The Jungle Book* to be read, I could immediately visualise the living room, my brother and I bawling our eyes out at a particularly sad part of *The Jungle Book*, and my father getting very angry because my mother had made us cry. She read us endless books and instilled in me a great love of reading, which did save my life a lot later on. When things got tough I'd go to the library at school and just read myself stupid with anything that I could pick up.

My father was an optometrist, but he was also a frustrated actor. He and his friends used to take part in local amateur dramatics, and the worst punishment that was ever meted out to me, when I put my brother's teddy bear in the copper, was that I wasn't allowed to go to his performance. I'd seen all the sets and a rehearsal. I was really furious. At the time I thought, 'I'll show you, I'll do my own.' Very early on if people said, 'No, you can't do that,' I would think. 'Why can't I do it?' I wouldn't take it easily.

My mother loved my father very deeply and I think it was a very passionate coupling. What really started to tip the scales was my younger brother's long illness and consequent death. My father never got over it. I was aware of the arguments even though they tried to hide them. I'd lie in bed at night and think, 'Oh Lord, what is happening to my world?' But they actually handled the break-up fairly well.

When I was about fifteen I was asked, 'Do you want to go with your mother or your father?' I thought, 'How dare anybody make me choose. I can't choose!' It made me very angry with both of them. I really didn't want to go with one or the other. I tried staying with my father for a while but it didn't work at all. It didn't work particularly well staying with my mother either but I was very fond of my brother and sister who were with her. We've always been very close.

I was packed off to boarding school. Before that I'd gone to a country high school in Moree. It was a coed school, which in fact gave me a very healthy attitude towards boys. When you grow up with boys you take them for granted. They're not special people. I had just as many boys as girls for friends at that coed school. We didn't get up to any nonsense. At least I didn't. Some of the others might have. I was a fairly dopey, naïve kid. I really liked a lot of the blokes in the class. They were great fun and did awful things like putting rockets through the roof. When I went to boarding school, which was all female, I couldn't believe that boys were things you talked about in hushed tones, and put on pedestals. I thought it was ridiculous. I was very glad that I had that coed education and I didn't send either of my kids to boarding school. I left school when I was seventeen. I got my Leaving Certificate but it wasn't a matriculation pass because I failed in maths. I was so unsettled because I didn't know quite where my loyalties lay. I still wanted that home and I still wanted my parents together.

Kids don't understand the emotions that parents go through and that sometimes the damage is too great. My parents didn't really speak to one another again until my father was quite ill. He went into a coma and the hospital advised me not to see him because it would upset me. My father aged twenty years in about three months and he didn't know where he was or what he was doing. He suddenly became another person. When he went into a coma my mother said to me, 'You should go to the hospital.' I was very angry with her and said, 'There's no point.' She went to the hospital and sat with him for about an hour and apparently just as she left he regained consciousness. One never knows the power of things like that. It was the only time he ever regained consciousness before he died. She said to me, 'He'll die on your birthday.' And he did. It was quite incredible. I found it all fairly shattering especially as my own marriage was breaking up at the same time. Fortunately I had two marvellous kids and they had become the most important things in my life. I honed in on them and their needs and that got me through.

I had a very strong-willed grandmother and my mother always accused me of being like her. It was supposed to be an insult. She was a very tough Englishwoman, who'd come out here when she was eleven as a foster-child to a really wealthy family in Tasmania. She had delusions of grandeur, and protocol was everything with her. To the day she died she had a full-length Union Jack in her bedroom. She always referred to England as home, and until I was seventeen or eighteen I thought that England was home and that I was here on sufferance. This was another reason for that lovely magic world within the paling fence round our backyard. I'm probably the only person who has ever had a sheltered upbringing in the western suburbs of Sydney. I wish I'd had some of the scrapes and problems that some of the other kids had. It probably would have made me more of a fighter much earlier and got me out of the self-indulgent shyness that I seemed to have.

I'm awful now because I do fight, if I feel I'm right. If my husband said to me, 'Oh, you can't do that,' I'd immediately set out to do it. I've often wished somebody had said to me,

If someone says I can't do it, I become absolutely determined . . . a remark like that does give you a sort of impetus.

'You'll never be able to play the piano,' because I'd have loved to play the piano. If someone says I can't do it, I become absolutely determined. When I was planning to make the film of *Picnic at Hanging Rock,* somebody said to me I'd never be able to put it together. Of course I didn't do it totally on my own. I had some very good people alongside me, and we all worked together. But a remark like that does give you a sort of impetus. We were knocked back so many times, but I still kept going. I have got a certain tenacity.

I've also always had a telepathic sense. I try and hide it or cut it out because I don't like it. I've often known when something's happened to very close friends. It scares me. I have friends who absolutely live at fortune-tellers, who won't move unless they know what's going on or whether their stars are right or not. I can't. I get in far too much of a bind. I do get flashes, especially about people. I suddenly have a distinct feeling that it is not sitting right. I have pulled out of situations because I've known that it's going to be a disaster, even if it meant losing over it. Yet I'm not able to put a finger on exactly what's worrying me until afterwards. I just know I'm unhappy. I think growing up in a household where there was a lot of hurt and a lot of joy made me aware of how people are feeling all the time. When we were doing *Beauty and the Beast* for Channel Seven we had some very good mind-reading people on the programme. We were all sitting up on the panel and I thought, I'm not going to let those two delve into my mind – no way.' I consciously pulled a blanket down. Afterwards this guy looked at me and said, 'You're one of us.' I thought, 'Well, I don't want to be,' and I just walked very quickly away. He knew I could control it. It's a bit frightening to know you have that power, so I really didn't do anything about it after that.

I was originally asked to join *Beauty and the Beast* because I seemed to be a gentle, happy little housewife. They needed that image because the rest of the panel were all divorcees or women who hadn't married. Four years later my marriage went by the board and my housewife image went right out the window. I don't think they knew what they were getting. Actually, because I was working with women who were supporting kids alone and who were having battles through the divorce courts, I tried to keep my marriage together longer. But when I was on my own with the kids, the show did provide me with a minor source of income and I made some of the best friends I've ever had on that panel.

I really wanted to be an archeologist. I used to read mystery stories until they were coming out of my ears and so many of them were set in old tombs and on archeological sites. I liked the discovery thing about archeology and the painstaking detective work people had to do. I went very briefly to Sydney University at night, and worked in the library during the day. But I didn't have the necessary stamina. I do now, I didn't then. So I joined the ABC as a clerk. That was a joke because I had no shorthand or typing skills. I know the personnel department were constantly wondering what to do with me. I'd be just about to get the sack and somebody would find a job for me.

Eventually I got a job in children's programmes, where I was forced to become an instant actress doing little parts and performing with very well established actors. It was as frightening as hell, but it was a tremendous challenge. I worked with really kind people who were ready to be patient with this hick. That's how I started performing. I had worked in the theatre before but mainly as a stage manager because I enjoyed putting things together. I worked very hard indeed in the studio and always tried to do my best, but I was fairly lazy outside the confines of work and I was a fairly lazy actress.

I was forced to do it otherwise I would have been sacked and my kids would not have been fed.

I had and still have a terror of going into a room full of people. I feel quite ill and often I don't go to things at the last minute. I can't face it. It's something I fight against and was helped in overcoming a bit when I did the *Today Show* for the Seven Network. There you were in a studio at seven in the morning having been up since five, suddenly faced with perfectly strange and highly intelligent people to interview. I got used to saying, 'How do you do, I'm Pat Lovell, I'll be talking to you, let's have a chat.' I was forced to do it because otherwise I would have been sacked and my kids would not have been fed.

When I went into television in 1957 I absolutely loved the

camera crews at the ABC. I learned more from them than I ever learned from a director. Nobody ever said anything more to me than, 'When the red light goes on, that's the camera you're talking to,' and 'Stop wrinkling your forehead,' and, 'Why don't you have your nose fixed?' That's terrific training to start a television career!

I stood solid in that resolve because I knew that the union of that book and Peter Weir were the important things.

When I was doing the *Today Show* and the film industry was emerging I seemed to be doing all the interviews. I was meeting people like Bruce Beresford and Phillip Adams, who were both heavily involved in the film industry. I wrote to Phillip about *Picnic at Hanging Rock* which I'd read and thought was highly visual, and he said, 'Why don't you do it? Why don't you produce it?' I said, 'I know nothing about production.' And he said, 'Well, I'll help you.' He really threw me in the deep end and I got a passion for that book and for making it into a film. And meeting Peter Weir was the luckiest thing. Some wretched clairvoyant at a party said, 'In 1973 your life changed because you had a business relationship with somebody, or an artistic relationship.' I said, 'Yes, it was Peter Weir, on *Picnic*.' Early in 1973 I'd gone round to him with the book. I had a terribly strong feeling about Peter even when he was floor assistant in Channel Seven peering at me from behind flats. He was a remarkable young man and I was watching the short films that he was making. When I saw *Homesdale* I was absolutely certain that he would be the person to direct *Picnic*. I stood solid in that resolve because I knew that the union of that book and Peter Weir were the important things. And that film was important for both him and for me. Later, Peter brought *Gallipoli* to me. He'd been working on it for a long time and I felt the same way about it.

The main problem for the Australian film industry has been our writers, but they are learning fast. We're getting better and better scripts. David Williamson is one of the most professional and talented writers I've ever had the pleasure of working with. The way he worked with Peter on *Gallipoli* was an eye-opener to me. And also Ken Cameron on *Monkey Grip*. Ken really slogged away. *Monkey Grip* was a book that was almost impossible to turn into a film and he really did it, head down, six drafts. He was still going while we were filming. It was a huge thing for him because it was his first feature and it was a really tough one. There are other good writers in this country, but I prefer not to name them at the moment because somebody else might nab them. Scripts have been our weak point, but I think that it will come good.

There are a lot of women now involved in the film industry and possibly a bigger percentage per head than anywhere else except in France. I think it's because when the industry restarted with government help and Phillip Adams and various other people in 1969, we weren't a male dominated industry. A lot of us had proven ourselves in other fields. I'd proven myself in the television field, Joan Long had proven herself as a writer and documentary-maker and Margaret Fink, the film producer, had proved herself as an intellectual and as a teacher. We didn't have to bow down to anybody. We came in on our own terms. Since then there've been quite a lot of people who have come in via production management and those areas. Women are good at organising things. They get a lot of experience organising their families and their lives. I think I can tell in an instant if things are not right.

If a woman has talent she'll get there. But she has to be willing to fight . . . to have tremendous determination and be single-minded about it.

If a woman has talent she'll get there. But she has to be willing to fight. I could easily have sat back with *Picnic* and said, 'Okay, you're bright organising boys, and Peter's the talented creative person, so I'm stepping out.' It probably would have saved me lots of sleepless nights. Naturally, because I'd fought for the thing for so long, I couldn't do it. In any case, I was absolutely fascinated that I knew so much from my years working in television and in the entertainment industry. You do pick up an awful lot of information, even though you think its useless at the time.

I watched and I thought, 'I *do* know how to organise a film!' You've got to have tremendous determination and be single-minded about it. From the time that *Picnic* was finished I was determined to prove myself as a sole producer. I moved straight into a film called *Break of Day*. I probably went into it too soon for the script to be right, but I don't regret that I made it. I learned a lot from producing it and Ken Hammond did a

> **You have to make tremendous sacrifices because you can't really have a private life in this business.**

lovely job of directing. The next year I went on to make *Summerfield*. Neither of those were box-office successes but I proved that I was a good creative producer. I had to bleeding-well prove it.

It's great when people say that they've enjoyed one of my films but I don't want fame as such because it's tough. Peter Weir now has international fame as a film director, and it is a hell of a thing to live up to. I'd hate to be put on that sort of pedestal. I still rather like being the quiet person – well, not so quiet, somebody said I was vociferous the other day – but being a person in the background. But you still have to be determined and fight. And you have to make tremendous sacrifices because you can't really have a private life in this business.

A male producer can easily have a wife. She can be of great help. But I don't want a man home in the kitchen. I enjoy cooking, sewing and gardening. I'm really very good at all those things that a lot of so-called 'free' women want to get out of. Most men over forty just want a nice quiet little girl who'll do everything for them. What they don't want is a fighting woman who goes off at a tangent to get things done, who would leave them standing looking slightly stunned for a period of time. My kids have been terribly understanding. I don't think having a berserk mother for a couple of years has really affected them. They've been tremendously supportive. We can be doing something quite normal at home when the phone will ring. I'll have to get into gear immediately and try and sort out the problem or else I'm on the phone for the rest of the day. There are times when I wonder if I'm lonely and then I don't have time to think about it. Sometimes I feel terribly lonely and I'll wallow for two days or so. Then I think 'You stupid bitch,' and remember how appalling I was at boarding school: how I used to cut people out, how self-indulgent I was, and how I used to withdraw and shut myself in the library and not speak to people for days. God help me if I ever go back to that.

An average day? I always set the alarm for quarter to seven. I'm optimistic, and try to get into gear fairly quickly. Usually the first thing I do is feed the animals which are either miaowing or

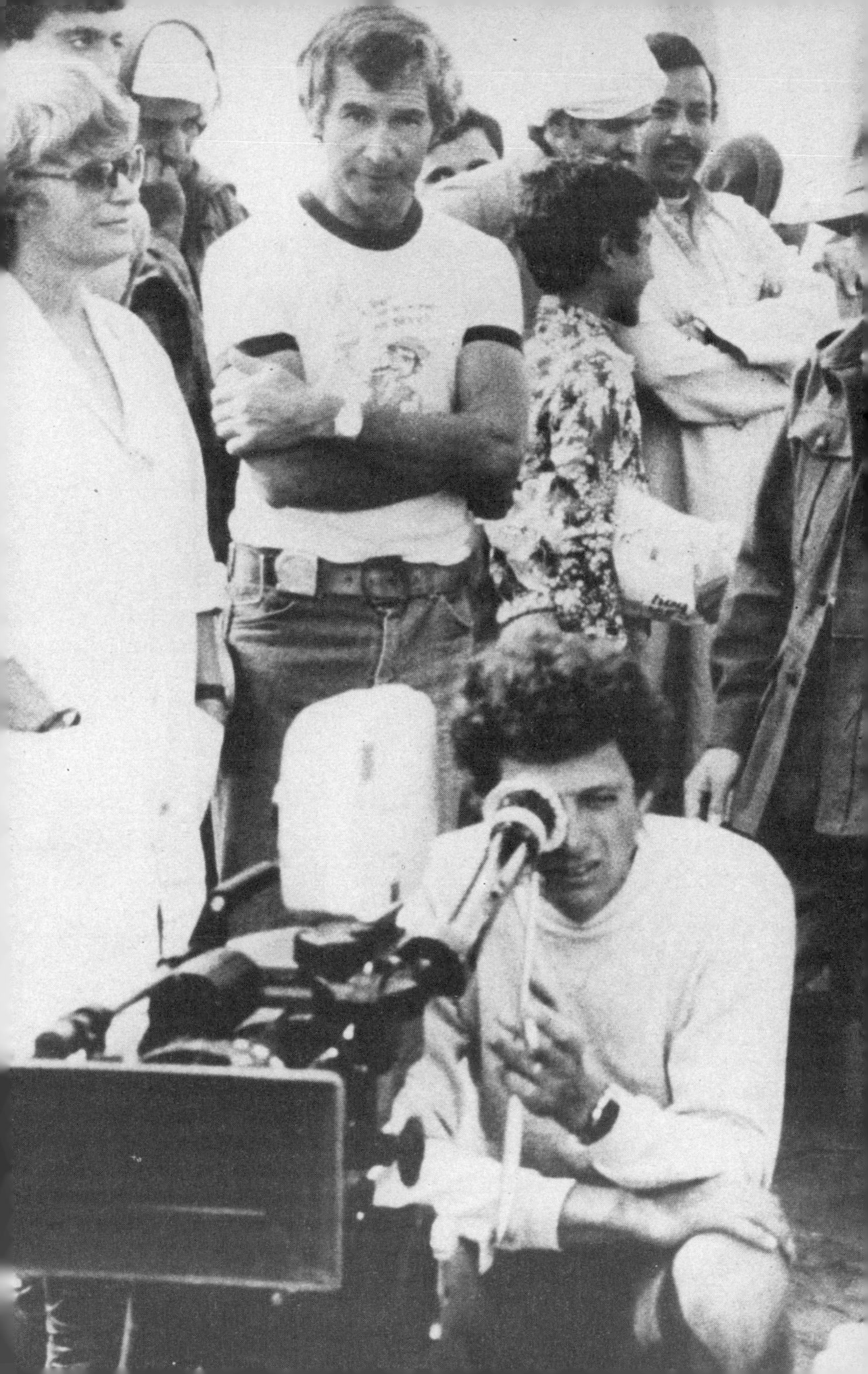

barking. Then I have a quick cup of tea and grapefruit and I'm usually in the car between eight-thirty and nine, having watered the garden and raced around. I have three-quarters of an hour to think in the car. I spend as much time as possible getting things sorted out at work and fortunately I have a good assistant who helps a lot. Just when you think you haven't got anything to do, suddenly everything happens. That's what the film business is like. Some days I go home so frustrated because I haven't been able to get everything done and other days I make four phone calls and everything goes into gear again. If I'm going out at night I go home twenty-five miles, feed the animals and come back. Otherwise, if I'm home on time, I usually watch the news and *Dr Who*, or I read. The minute I get home I find the mantle of worry falling off. It's so peaceful here by the water.

I always felt I should become this capable or this competent at something . . . so that I am accepted as a person and not as a woman.

I don't know whether I'm a feminist or not. Some years ago I joined Media Women, an organisation that Germaine Greer was involved in. I made a lot of friends with women who worked in radio or as journalists. I guess I've been scared off by a lot of really rampaging feminists who don't have a good thing to say about blokes. I've always worked very happily alongside men and I just can't make the divisions. They're all people to me. I've had problems with some chaps who have obviously been dead against me because I'm a woman. There's no point in really talking to them. We have to try and work together on another sort of angle. I probably haven't worked feminism out. I know I'm a woman, but to me it's not a big issue at all. Because I haven't been living with anyone I'm not forced to confront it.

I must admit I haven't done very much for the social standing of women, although *Monkey Grip* does to a certain extent because it makes the highly optimistic statement that the mother and child relationship is the strongest of all. And when you've got that, then to hell with the rest. Helen Garner worked out a lot of things for me when she wrote that book. I wish I'd reached her understanding at thirty-three. I try not to think too much about myself and how I feel. I've blocked a lot of it out. One of the reasons I made *Monkey Grip*, apart from the fact that it is a wonderful starring vehicle for a woman, is that it explores women's weaknesses when they fall physically in love, what they do and how far they go to try and keep that love. And it's about today. *Monkey Grip* has been seen by many French people who are fascinated by the film because it's the first time they've seen modern Australia. It's getting a very good reaction.

I don't ever deride the women's movement. It's probably the most important thing that's happened to women all around the world because it's given us some hope of equality. I should admit that in the radio and television days I always felt that I had to be so much better than a man to do it. There are millions of mediocre men but there aren't many mediocre women around in business. They can't afford to be. In the film industry there's still that sneaking feeling that you've got to be that much better. But if that's what you've got to do, you do it. I always felt I should become this capable or this competent at something so that I can hold my own anywhere, so that I am accepted as being a person and not as a woman.

But I think women have brought a lot of problems on themselves. I know that's blaming the victim, but we've got to take some of the blame. Mothers indulge their sons in this country. I've indulged my son as well, but I hope living with two women has given him more understanding, I've noticed that in England or France mothers have a very different attitude towards their sons. The men are much more polite and much more understanding. Maybe they're just the same bastards underneath, who knows? One day Annie Deveson and I were sitting around decrying the fact that we were single women, loved by no man at that time. Anne said, 'I think Australian men are scared off by women who appear intelligent.' And I said, 'Well, I don't think I'm that intelligent but possibly I appear so because I do fight for what I want.' And she said, 'Yes, I think you frighten the life out of a lot of Austalian men.' I've come to the conclusion that maybe I do. Is that the price of success?

When she had recounted a painful incident from her childhood where her mother had mistaken an inability to cope with grief as insensitivity, Pat had wept. Such is her dedication to truth that she was prepared to allow the past to hurt her again. Glimpses such as these helped me understand why at the end of the interview I knew that she wanted me to leave quickly. It was as if she had allowed herself to be

vulnerable and wanted to get back under her carapace again.

Just before my taxi arrived she said, 'I don't really want to think about myself. I just want to work and produce good films. I don't want to sit still and think. I'm still wallowing. I hope I haven't said anything that might hurt people. There's been enough hurt in my life.'

PAT O'SHANE (Head of NSW Department of Aboriginal Affairs)

I felt rather daunted by the prospect of meeting someone with so many 'firsts' to her name. Pat O'Shane was the first Aboriginal woman to become a teacher in Queensland, the first Aboriginal to become a lawyer in Australia and she was the first woman ever to be appointed to the Metropolitan Water, Sewerage and Drainage Board.

Her cheerful, smiling face almost lulled me into believing that things couldn't have been all that tough for Pat O'Shane.

As the afternoon slipped by and we sipped away at a few white wines, I could hardly believe the harshness of the life that was being unfolded before me. The tears were in my eyes, not hers. She has come too far and fought too hard to be caught in the trap of self-pity or martyrdom. When she told me she had been sent to Sydney to undergo psychosurgery, I was so taken aback that with child-like naïvety I stammered, 'You didn't have it, did you?' 'Well, I'd hardly be sitting here talking to you if I had, would I?' The response was not unkind, merely ironic.

When I was in primary school, kids used to take flowers to the teacher. By Friday afternoon they'd be just about wilted, but the teacher would give the flowers to one of the kids in the class to take home for the weekend. I used to turn myself inside out to be one of the good students, but I never got the flowers. It wasn't until years later that I realised that the reason I didn't get them was because I was the outsider. I feel very resentful about it in retrospect. I've always talked a lot and laughed a

lot, but when I was younger I used to feel a lot of hurt. My mother told me that I often came home in tears.

As a child, my role, which was imposed by my parents, was to protect my younger sister and brothers from the kind of barbs that they got from people. I did that. I had to repress whatever I felt and really be that strong person. I thought, 'I will use this as a spur,' and it's worked. Now when I go back to Cairns for holidays, people greet me – people I went right through school with who never spoke to me in those days. Today they greet me down the street because now it's nice to know Pat O'Shane. I'm very cynical about that but I can afford to smile at them and be friendly. I can afford to be generous now, can't I?

When I was in grade six in primary school I topped the class. A boy who had come top in the previous term exams was my main competition. I'll never forget this day. The teacher said to him, 'You should be ashamed of yourself letting a girl beat you.' I thought 'He's never going to beat me again.' And he never did. That teacher had quite a thing about maths not being a girl's subject. Even when I was in intermediate (in those days in Queensland, we had intermediate before secondary) the teacher told us that science wasn't a girl's subject. Yet that was really what I was most interested in and good at.

It wasn't until after I was married that I went back to secondary school and did my science courses. I actually did a two-year physics course in seven days and nights, got a B in the junior examination, went on to technical college and topped the class. I never did anything with that qualification. I just wanted to develop my interest in it and prove to myself that I could do it. I suppose I've never undertaken anything that I didn't really feel I was going to succeed in.

I was born in a tiny sugar town, probably the northernmost sugar town in Australia, about fifty miles north of Cairns in Queensland. My mother didn't have an education. I think she went to grade three in primary school. She was Aboriginal. My father was Irish, very well-travelled and well-educated. He cut cane in the sugar fields around Mossman. When I was old enough to go to school the family moved to Cairns so that I could get an education. There were five of us altogether and I was the first born, named Patricia, shortened to Pat all of my life. I've been reading lately that short sharp names are action names. In Queensland you're either black or you're white. No half-way measures. It didn't ever enter my head that I could 'pass for white', which was something that was put to me when, at the age of thirty-two, I first came to live in Sydney. I found it quite horrifying, because in Queensland I'd never ever been anything but Aboriginal. Even though my father was white and we didn't live on a reserve, he was ostracised by his workmates, and he found it difficult to get accommodation for his family.

One of the things I used to see in Queensland in particular, but I've seen it in other parts of the country as well, was that whenever there was an inter-racial liaison with a white man, the woman would often walk well behind the man. She was usually treated very badly. I can honestly say that my father never did that. He treated my mother with the very greatest respect. They were two people who truly loved each other. I admired my father very much on account of this. He stood by his wife and his family against all those kinds of odds which must have been difficult for him to cope with. They married in 1940 and attitudes were a long way behind those of today. Even now they're not too good. There was no such thing as a guaranteed wage in those days. I can remember my father working from seven in the morning till seven at night, from the time I was about three years old. As an Irish trade union militant my father taught me to always question authority. He certainly gave me bite.

The driving thing was for me to get an education to get out of the poverty that we lived in . . . My mother always used to say that we were as good as anyone else.

My mother was quite a tall woman, about five feet ten-and-a-half inches and very athletic. I always saw her running and swimming. She was very alive and she looked beautiful. People would stop her in the street to tell her how good she looked. She had enormous pride and dignity. I'll give you an example. Dad had joined an organisation they used to call the Royal Order of Buffaloes or something, a lodge. He took Mum along to a dance and this chap asked her to dance with him. Of course the dance floor was crowded with people and her partner said to her, 'You have interesting blood in you, what is it?' She said, 'I'm Australian Aboriginal.' He left her right there standing on the dance floor. That's the kind of experience she had to ride. She had many of those in her lifetime. Yet it didn't make her a bitter person. She just had to become tough to survive that kind of thing. Those who aren't tough go under. I think alcoholism is one manifestation of that. From her I got the knowledge that we are as good as anybody else and we can show them that we are. Her courage was amazing. I have enormous pride in our people and I never fail to tell everyone that. I suppose I've got a lot of pride in myself too.

When I started seconday school, my mother worked as a domestic in hotels around town. She was a very intelligent person and always drummed it into me and the other kids that we really had to get an education. I can recall times when Dad was on strike and there was no food. We had to go to school without breakfast. We'd come home and gather pippies on the beach or go fishing, having been at school all day without any food. My parents went without lots of meals so that we could eat a little to keep us going to school. That's why I'm where I am today. The driving thing was for me to get an education to get out of the poverty that we lived in.

My mother's parents came off the Argyle, which was the Church of England mission established at the turn of the century under the provisions of the Queensland so-called Protection Act at the time. My grandfather had to get his exemption for the family to get off the reserve. Once the male head of a family received exemption, the whole family went off. But even until 1972 the Act contained provisions that if somebody in authority deemed that an Aboriginal person was not a fit and proper person to be living in the general community, then that person could be taken back to a reserve. My grandfather had worked so hard to get the family off the reserve, and he always insisted that we behave properly so that we would never be taken back. Even though my father was white and neither my mother or I had ever lived on a reserve, that provision would have applied to me as well, because I was deemed to be Aboriginal under the terms of the Act. By the time I was fifteen I was the only Aboriginal in our vicinity who had ever read the Act right through, and I wrote a critique of it. I became very political, which was always part of our upbringing. My mother had been a member of the Aborigines' Advancement League that was established at that time. I became involved and used it to inform members of the organisation and to work out some kind of political actions around the Queensland Act.

There weren't many Aboriginal kids at my school. In my class in lower primary school I think there was one other Aboriginal girl and a couple of boys. They were guys who've made names for themselves in the Aboriginal affairs scene: Bob Mathers who worked with the Aboriginal Affairs Department for a while and Ray Majors who worked with Aboriginal hostels. I was the first one ever to go right through secondary school in North Queensland. We lived in a tent with a dirt floor. We didn't have running water. I knew that we lived in different circumstances from the other kids at school. They all lived in houses for a start. I was used to kids calling me black gin and black nigger, which you would probably find hard to believe looking at me, but that was my experience at school. I often had physical fights – black eyes, bloody nose, that kind of thing. By the time I got to secondary school what I used to do with my fists I started doing with my tongue. By that time I had proved I was acceptable. I was school captain. I could swim like a fish. I could run for miles. I represented Queensland in zone sports.

But I knew I was different. I was regarded as a pretty aggressive sort of person. To this day men tell me that I'm a very aggressive woman. I'm not a vindictive person. I never have been. I try to find ways of changing the system which makes people like they are. I try to be understanding of people's attitudes. Sometimes there are some people who are simply lost causes, and it's not worth my while spending any time on them. But I don't harbour grudges.

I had three brothers and we all took turns to carry the water, to get up early in the morning and chop the wood and light the fire and, if we were lucky, to cook the porridge for breakfast. There was no such thing as women's work and men's work. When you live in the bush you're really doing it the hard way. But it was a different thing once I got into the broader community. I could never accept the secondary status of women. Both my mother and father used to tell me that I was just as capable of achieving as the boys. I believed them.

I made up my mind that I wasn't going to be a typist or a nurse. My father tried to persuade me to become a nurse as it was regarded as being a very good job for Aboriginal women. There was only one at the time – Dulcie Reading who became

> **I told him I was going to work for ever and he said that was fine by him. After we were married he said no wife of his was going to work . . . I was absolutely appalled.**

Dulcie Farr. She later came to Sydney and is now working with the Aboriginal Medical Service in Redfern. She was thought to have hit a pinnacle because she had become a nurse. I looked around at what options were available. I'd always been interested in doing medicine but because I wasn't doing science that was out. I heard about teachers' scholarships so I applied for one and got it. I'd done very well in my junior examinations. I was fifteen. It took six months for them to actually send it through. This became a political issue and was raised in parliament.

I was the first Aboriginal female to become a teacher in Queensland. Mick Miller, the guy I later married, was the first Aboriginal teacher to come from Palm Island. We met at teachers' college. There weren't any others for a considerable number of years afterwards. I was actually teaching in secondary school by the time the next Aboriginal students were going through teachers' college. Very few people hung on long enough. They didn't have the motivation in that kind of system. It was very difficult. The Queensland Government were pretty nice to Mick. They wined and dined him. He met Princess Alexandra and even danced with her. He stayed at the home of Dr Noble who was then Minister for Native Affairs, as it was in those days. Mick really couldn't see anything wrong with the system.

I thought he had some pretty good ideas because when I told him that I was going to work for ever he said that was fine by him. After we were married he said no wife of his was going to work, that we were going to have half a dozen children and a wife's place was in the kitchen. I was absolutely appalled. I said to him, 'But we talked about these kinds of things before we were married and you didn't indicate then that was your attitude.' If I'd known that, I'd never have married. It became a very serious source of conflict between us. I did go to work; I had only two children and I worked virtually from the time that they were born. Mick had different ideas about what women ought to be doing. He certainly felt that very strongly. I think I had a politicising effect on him. That's pretty obvious seeing him today as President of the North

Queensland Land Council. He jetsets all over the world and he riles Bjelke Petersen, but in those days he never rocked the boat. He used to tell me that I shouldn't do the things that I was involved in. He could never see what I was on about, but through our involvement in schools he was forced to confront racist attitudes. There were parents around Cairns who did not want their kids to be taught by Mr Miller and he had never had to take that kind of thing before. That really had an effect on him, but he still had this attitude about women. To my mind he had limited life goals and I had very broad ones. I had horizons to conquer.

I used to have my battles royal in the teaching profession. I remember teachers referring to the Aboriginal kids in the school, most of whom were in special classes for slow learners, as 'boongs'. I had a class of Aboriginal girls and one day one of the teachers referred to them as black sluts. Some of their parents came around to visit me that night at home. I took up that issue with the teacher the next day. Instead of having the guts to stand up and have the issue out with me he complained to the principal. The principal carpeted me at the next staff meeting. Not being a shrinking violet i aired the entire issue and let the whole staff know the facts. The teacher and the principal were sorry that they had ever opened their mouths to me. Another day I had a big argument with one of the women in my staffroom. Her husband had actually been at teachers' college with Mick. They were good mates and played in the same cricket team and basketball team. She was telling me that Aboriginal kids were ineducable past the age of fifteen. I said, what about Mick and myself? She told me that we were different.

In my greatest hour of need he said, 'No.' I said, 'Well, I'm never coming back' . . . He made his choice, but so did I.

But not all whites were bad. Even in that very small community we had a mixture of friends. Most of us played a lot of sport, which was a source of interest, and people socialised within those kinds of areas. Our political views may not have coincided but that was of no great moment in that kind of community. But it wasn't enough for me in the long run.

I taught ten-and-a-half years altogether. Then I had a breakdown. All the problems that I'd been repressing came to the surface. That was a very traumatic experience for me. It went on for about four years. Finally I was recommended to undergo psychosurgery and was referred to Sydney. I asked Mick to come with me. I really needed somebody to support me. I was in a very, very bad way. He couldn't take having an 'insane' wife. It was a source of shame to him. In my greatest hour of need he said, 'No.' I said, 'Well, I'm never coming back,' and I never did. I've just gone on to better things. I'm never going back down into those dark depths again. He made his choice, but so did I.

By the time the psychiatrists and mental institutions had finished with me, I was pretty well a physical wreck. At one stage I did almost die in hospital and it took a long, long time to recover from that. I can't tell you the horrors I went through. I do a lot of work for mentally-ill people. Enormous work has to be done in those areas, like protection of civil rights. I'm not completely obsessive about it. I know that people have problems and go through behavioural patterns which are very difficult for others to cope with. But I don't think that the administration of the kinds of drugs and electroconvulsive therapy, which I had masses of, helps people to get out of that. In fact, I think they tend to aggravate the condition. But I never did undergo the psychosurgery. Otherwise you wouldn't be talking to me today, would you?

My children were partly with Mick and partly with me. They knew I was very ill. They were gentle little kids. I had been in and out of hospital as an outpatient and they knew that there was something wrong with mummy. That was a trauma to me as well, but once I got on my feet again, and the divorce proceedings went through, I had them with me. For most of the next seven years I had one and Mick had one, but I wasn't very happy with that arrangement, so I applied for full custody and got it. We're three happy women now. Of course we have our fights, but on the whole we really like each other.

I did actually have a little money in the bank when I came to Sydney. I just worked around the city in secretarial jobs for about twelve months. I was very ill, very thin and I was crying a lot. I couldn't cope very well, but I got involved in the black moratorium and the setting up of the tent embassy in Canberra. I met Hal Wotten who was then Dean of the Faculty of Law at the University of New South Wales (UNSW). I talked to him about doing Law, because I really did think that I could do it. It had been in my mind for about ten years. Back in Cairns,

the organisation I was in had become involved in a case of two Aboriginal women, one of whom was only fifteen, who'd been beaten up by a couple of police officers. They'd gone on to the reserve and broken into the small huts, raped one of the women and badly beaten the other. The women laid charges against them. That court case lasted for eleven days and those men were convicted. The court of sessions, or whatever it was called in those days, upheld that conviction but they only got two years in prison with hard labour. Both of them of course were discharged from the police force. I sat through all of that and when the judge brought down his decision I remember the police breaking down and crying. I thought two years in prison was nothing compared to the kinds of things that they used to inflict on Aboriginal people.

I realised that we needed a lawyer ourselves. That idea preyed on my mind for years but it wasn't until I came to Sydney that it really gelled. I just knew that I was the person who could do it. I was admitted to the UNSW Law School as a graduate. It was a hard slog. I did secretarial work in school holidays and university vacations. I also had an Aboriginal study grant of about twenty-six dollars a week. What really got me through was posting photographs of my mother, who had died many years before, on the wall with little slogans saying, 'She did it, I can do it.' Sometimes that was the only thing that kept me going.

After graduating as a lawyer, I went straight to the bar here in Sydney and into private practice. It was the hard way to go, like jumping in the deep end feet first. I got a lot of briefs from the Aboriginal Legal Service here in Redfern and one from the Royal Commission into New South Wales prisons. Then I went up to Alice Springs where they decided that they wanted an Aboriginal female lawyer and since I was the first and only Aboriginal lawyer at the time, they thought it would be great if I went up there.

I find it difficult to say I'm black first and a woman second or vice versa. I can't make that kind of distinction. Amongst Aboriginal women I do my best to raise their consciousness both as women and as Aboriginals. For instance, one morning when I

Authorities have ignored Aboriginal women's views on a whole range of issues. It's part of my job to try to reverse that.

was working with the Aboriginal Legal Aid in Alice Springs where the other lawyers were white, I heard one of these guys ask one of the office typists, who were all Aboriginal, to make him a cup of coffee. I stormed in and said, 'What's going on here? If this is going to be the situation then we'd better go on a roster. Everybody gets to make the coffee in turn, otherwise we make our own.' That was the first time that it had ever been put to those guys. It was also the first time it had ever been put to those women. Not that I didn't have problems with black men as well, particularly in the early days of the black movement. Black sexual politics had never been discussed, let alone documented, and that was really difficult. I was clearly a threat. I think I've got a fairly good political mind. I wasn't after media attention like a lot of those guys were. I think they tended to respond too much to media flattery.

The late '60s, early '70s were fairly heady days. A whole range of people were going to lead Australia, lead the entire world. It was quite a threat to those black radicals to confront a black woman who was articulate, analytical, political, who put forward all kinds of working programmes but more importantly, actually got in there and did some hard work – you know, type the stencils, run them off, distribute them, talk at meetings and still have some kind of direction and get on with other things as well. Not that it was any different from the problems the white women were having with the white men in the left. It was the same old line, 'You can make the coffee but we'll make the decisions and speak to the media.' One chap here in Sydney was getting a lot of media coverage, but was conspicuous by his absence when it came to the hard grind. At one meeting when the media were all there, television cameras in the back of the room, he suddenly came striding in about to make a big show. We'd been discussing these issues for a while. He came in and said, 'Note this.' I turned around and said, 'Who the fuck are you? Where were you yesterday when we were writing those stencils and running them off, distributing them, talking at those meetings, tramping the city, out doing the hard yakka? We've made some decisions. You're not coming in and overturning them or that democratic process.' It was the first time in his life that he had ever been challenged, certainly by a woman. I'd just had enough. He was struck dumb.

Two of those men bailed me up in Redfern one night. I thought it was going to be just about the end of me. They started screaming at me, which was interesting, they didn't hit me. Mind you, they wouldn't have wanted to. With my background I was capable of hitting back. I just told them to get fucked, hailed the first cab and off I went. They've never treated me like that again.

Maybe I'm being too harsh, but I think Australian men – black and white – are basically misogynists . . . It's a bit sad. Still I figure it's their loss.

One of the interesting aspects of that whole era was that a lot of them were really standing over the women and insisting that those women fuck them in order to be part of their little power clique. That was something I wasn't into either. I had my personal integrity to look after. I've never made sexual deals with any of them – black, white or brindle. As far as I'm concerned, I get there on my merit. It doesn't worry me if I don't get there if the price is screwing with those guys to give them another notch in their belts. It's quite an elusive game, because I know women who screwed with guys in power positions who have still missed out. So ultimately there's nothing in it, at least for women. I knew that instinctively from a long way back. But it really caused me a lot of problems in terms of trying to work within black organisations around here in particular. Not only did I get that kind of flack from the men but I also got it from other women. It hurt me a lot because I really thought that they were people that I could depend on. But you know the way in which sexual politics works and the way men play off one woman against another or one group of women against another. I think it's something we've not really come to terms with even today in lots of ways. But that was okay. Ultimately the women came round and in fact they're my main source of support.

I haven't remarried. I get a lot of support from my friends. I did live with a guy for a few years, but that turned out to be a fairly negative experience. He became extremely jealous of my achievements. I always vowed I'd never live with a white guy, but I did. I thought he was a very intelligent person. But he hadn't completed secondary school education and his jealousy of my achievements created a lot of problems. Interestingly enough, he took up law and is doing very well. A lot of men see me in the mother role. A lot of them see me as a threat. I have no doubt about that. They say that they see me as a strong, independent woman. Then they want to get involved with me. I'll go out to dinner and I might even go to bed with them. Then I get this line like, 'Oh, you're too independent, you're too this, you're too that.' I get very angry about that because it means that they don't accept me as a person. I'm always prepared to accept them as ordinary human beings. On the whole, Australians are a fairly lazy kind of people in terms of putting their heads into gear. Maybe I'm being too harsh, but I think Australian men – black and white – are basically misogynists. They just cannot relate to me as an intelligent, articulate, human being. I have my soft spots and my very tender parts, but I've learned not to reveal them to men, because they use them. That's caused me pain in the past. It's a bit sad. Still, I figure it's their loss.

I'm established now. I've proved myself. I certainly went through a very tough testing period. Men used to come along especially to rattle me. I'd be invited to speak at conferences and seminars and I told the truth. I didn't deviate. I said the things they would have said if they could have. I didn't ever compromise my principles about the issues. I'm honest about my political commitment. I'm not going to be bought off and I don't sell out. I don't consider that because I've been successful I should turn my back on people, which is something that's been put to me often in interviews. You know the line that goes, 'Now you're just part of the white bureaucracy.' I haven't lost contact with my grassroots people. They ring me up and say, 'We've got this problem. What can you do about it? What can we do about it?' My advice is sought on a whole range of issues. They know I'm in there trying to work to improve the situation.

I'm not going to be bought off and I don't sell out. I don't consider that because I've been successful I should turn my back on people.

When I returned to Sydney I went back to the bar, then on to Rozelle as an advocate. I went to Law School, did a bit of part time tutoring and research, and was also able to continue with private practice. I did a lot of work gratis because I was on a salary at the university. Then I got a job with the New South

Wales Parliamentary Select Committee, which meant virtually an end to any active practice of law. I did a lot of legal work, but of a different kind. More recently I went to the Office of Women's Affairs. I think it is important to try to work within the bureaucracy but for a long time I resisted going into it. I've been offered all kinds of government positions throughout the country, and I've always refused them because I thought my job was really out in the grassroots organisations. But there are a lot of people now who can do that work, and there aren't many people who have my qualifications and competence to do the kind of work that I'm doing now. I do think it's important for me to open up avenues for other Aboriginal people within those areas that I'm working in. For example, the Office of Women's Affairs is establishing a task force on Aboriginal women and their needs, because that's something that has not been done in this country. Ideally there ought to be an Aboriginal women's grassroots organisation that could do that, but the system works against people being able to do that kind of thing. They need massive financial resources just to get around to meetings. People live in such isolated areas in the country, and Australia's a big country. Our airfares are prohibitive these days. Authorities have ignored Aboriginal women's views on a whole range of issues. It's part of my job to try to reverse that.

I'm a talker. I'll talk for ever and a day. When I go to public meetings and demonstrations and things like that, people tell me that they've built up libraries of tapes of all the talks that I've given. Sometimes I wish I had taped myself. It's only in the last three years that I've had some sense of my own history, and the knowledge that I've actually forged a way for a lot of other Aboriginal women. I go round the country and Aboriginal women come up to me – women that I've never seen before and I'm never likely to see again, women who are really traditionally-oriented and who are fairer than I am even. They put their arms around me and greet me and tell me what I've done for them. That really makes me feel good. I feel as if I'm home when they tell me that.

I was aware of how often Pat used the pronoun 'I', and how she said it with such toughness and determination. Tough she certainly was. Nobody or nothing would ever destroy her belief in herself. She was a tall poppy who had been cut

down to the roots and, having bloomed again, God help anyone who ever tried to cut her down. When she left she said there was a job she'd like to get – the Head of the Department of Aboriginal Affairs in New South Wales.

Yet another first was added to the list. Having been appointed she had to confront the controversy over the New South Wales Land Rights Legislation. I heard her on a morning radio programme. The strong, clear voice was unmistakable. It's not easy being a black woman at the top of a white bureaucracy. I rang her recently to ask what the hardest part of her new job had been.

'Dealing with chauvinist males who are threatened by a woman having this much power.'

'Black or white men?'

'Mostly black, unfortunately.'

'How do you cope with that?'

'It doesn't affect me unduly. Women have always been my support and power base. They know the score. I wouldn't have survived without them.'

Acknowledgements

The South Australian College of Advanced Education provided a research grant for me to cover some of the expenses of the interviews. I thank them for their belief in the project.

The women of the Registry of the Magill Campus typed the manuscript and particular thanks must go to Ursula Burchett and Meg Burchell. My friends and colleagues Maureen Dyer, Lindy Powell, Rosemary Wighton, Jill Maling and Peggy Mares all read parts of the manuscript and gave me enthusiastic and positive reinforcement.

My thanks to Bruce Sims and Julie Watts for their sensitive and sympathetic editing. It was Mary Beasley whose energy, inspiration, bullying and love kept me going.

My thanks to the Woodhead Sisters who were always the 'tall poppies' in the family, and finally, my thanks to the women in the book who allowed themselves to be open to such close and intense questioning.

Quoted material: Extract from Simone de Beauvoir, *The Second Sex*, Penguin Books, 1972, p. 29 (this translation by H. M. Parshley first published by Jonathan Cape, 1953).

Photographs: All photographs are from private collections with the exception of p. 58, The *Age*, Melbourne, 9 January 1973; p. 77, Shanahan Management Pty Ltd, Sydney; pp. 84 and 87, Sydney Theatre Company Ltd; p. 143, The *Bulletin*, Sydney, 30 November 1982.

Photograph on p. 8 by John Scott; p. 13 by Tara Heinemann; p. 21 by Peter Leiss; p. 39 by Warren Kirkness; p. 115 by Helmut Newton; p. 130 by John Pearson; p. 153 by Elaine Kitchener.

ALSO AVAILABLE IN PENGUIN

Winning Women

Challenging the Norms in Australian Sport

Susan Mitchell and Ken Dyer

From the beginning women have been told that sport is unfeminine and that through sport their bodies would become musclebound, destroying their chances of marriage and wrecking their ability to have children.

In *Winning Women* Susan Mitchell asks thirteen sporting champions how they resolved the conflict between their roles as women and as sports stars. Despite bans and restrictions, women have excelled in swimming, athletics, squash, tennis, shooting, horse racing, cycling, car rallying and drag racing but, considered unnewsworthy, they are rarely seen playing sport on television.

Analysing the dilemmas facing sporting women, Susan Mitchell and Ken Dyer discuss the part played by drugs and explore the issue of women competing against men.

• Dawn Fraser • Raelene Boyle • Heather McKay • Evonne Cawley • Petra Rivers • Bev Francis • Donna Gould • Glynis Nunn • Sylvia Muehlberg • Bev Buckingham • Marlene Mathews • Wendy Ey • Helen Menzies.

Fathers at Home

Jan Harper

A father: Giving up work was a 'big decision, because I felt I was losing my ego. I felt there was no status, being home with the children.' A mother: 'I often used to come home and see that the house looked untidy, and think "What *have* you been doing all day?"'

The men and women who have contributed to *Fathers at Home* consciously challenged the father-breadwinner and mother-housewife traditions: the mothers worked outside the home, and the fathers cared for the children and did housework. In reviewing their experiences, Jan Harper examines the social and psychological implications, the rewards and difficulties, of their setting out on this unconventional path.

Despite the problems and uncertainties, the parents could say: 'we have learnt a lot about ourselves, and far more than simply the mechanics of caring for a baby.' We 'have found more pleasing life-styles, to carry us into the future.'

Nothing to Spare

Jan Carter

Nothing to Spare presents a series of sensitively etched portraits of women who have experienced nearly a century of Australia's history. Drawing on their own evocative accounts, Jan Carter reaches into the lives of women whose situations range from a butcher's daughter who delivered each of her seventeen children alone in a tent to a bishop's daughter who took her upper-class position for granted.

Their memories reveal vividly the society of the times – in the outback, on the goldfields, in the city – and offer rich insights into their roles and identity, their aspirations and relationships.

This book is more than a collection of reminiscences by particular people at a particular time: it implies that women who are now forgotten and isolated because they are old have powerful messages for us, when they are allowed to speak. They challenge us to reassess our own lives and values, and especially our attitudes towards old people.

There's No Place Like Home

Mary Leunig

A highly original collection of coloured drawings reflecting the fears, frustrations and fantasies of the artist, mostly as wife and mother in the domestic situation. In turn satirical, poignant, blackly comical, wistful, naughty, whimsical and plain funny, this fantastic journal reveals some of the absurd truths about everyday experiences that many women can identify with.

Mary Leunig's work has appeared in a number of magazines, including *Nation Review* (not to be confused with the cartoons of her brother, Michael), *Cleo, Forum, Penthouse* and *Matilda.*